AT GALACTIC CENTRAL

THE TRAVELS OF SCOUT SHANNON

KATE MACLEOD

1

SCOUT SHANNON CLIMBED in a steady rhythm, efficient but not so quick as to leave her short of breath. Life on Amatheon had very seldom called for climbing, so it was a new skill for her. One that would have come in handy back when she was on Schneeheim.

But it had taken coming to Galactic Central, the urban heart of the known universe, for Scout to really hone the ability to scale rock faces.

She had climbed this particular slope more than any other, and her muscle memory was so good she didn't even have to look for handholds anymore. Her fingers already knew where to find them, and her toes knew every gap large enough to serve as a step.

At last, she reached the top, pulled herself up onto the narrow ledge, then flopped down. She pushed the fog-wet hair from her face, drew in a deep breath of the oxygen-rich air that still carried the thick green smell of the plants that had created it, and looked around.

No one should be looking her way, not when she was clinging to the outer wall of one of the many citadels that floated on islands remote from each other in this part of the cloud. But Daisy had pressed upon her the importance of always being vigilant, and Scout had taken the lesson to heart.

She looked carefully from island to island, the reflective lenses of her glasses automatically changing range to bring each up in sharp detail before she turned her attention to the next, an island closer or further away. Some were walled all around like her current perch; nothing much to see there. Others were built in elegant terraces, level after level of gardens with small buildings dotted among the plant life. One consisted entirely of trees, immense trees with trunks hundreds of meters across. The human structures on that island were hidden among the leafy canopy, just a bridge or walkway visible here and there where the foliage was sparser.

She kind of wanted to explore that place someday. Not that she'd ever get the chance. All these islands were the private property of trade dynasties. Trade dynasties who had entire armies of security people to keep the riffraff at bay.

Scout knew the owner of the wall she was crouching on and had his permission to be there, but even still she kept out of sight, only scaling as far up the wall as was necessary to see into the gardens of one of the terraced islands.

Today she was early. No one was walking the paths yet. She reached into her pockets and pulled out a pair of gloves, then snuggled deeper into her jacket to wait. The vegetable smell of the air was so thick it was coating the back of her throat like she was growing moss of her own back there. She tucked her nose inside her zipped-up collar, breathing in the more pleasant yet faint smell of her dogs that always lingered in her clothes.

They would be missing her. They hated being alone. But there was no way to bring them with her.

She didn't think they'd understood when she'd explained it. Well, she'd make it up to them just as soon as they left this place.

The constant wind was chilling, especially wet as she was from her trip through the fog, and the stone beneath her resisted her body's attempt to warm it. The larger floating islands closer to the center of the cloud contained their own warmer atmosphere, drier and less prone to shearing winds. Scout supposed the homes on these islands had something similar. The people she saw in the gardens seemed perfectly comfortable in shirt sleeves, their long hair flowing softly behind them with only the slightest ripples from gentle breezes.

Outside the walls it was different, the opposite of warm and sheltering. But at least she could breathe. She could ignore any amount of cold and wet; she was even growing used to it and rather liked that first touch of it when she stepped out in the morning, that first lungful that made her shiver but brought her sleepy brain to full awareness.

But not having to wear a mask while she was climbing was a bonus she never stopped being grateful for.

A flicker of motion caught her eye, and she sat up straighter, letting her glasses bring the scene into detail for her. She still had no implant, but the glasses were smart. They were learning to anticipate her needs to a degree where she seldom had to make a verbal command.

She intently watched the section of path that emerged from between two trees with long, sweeping, leaf-covered branches. The trees stood to either side of the door that opened out from the side of the enormous citadel that sat atop the highest terrace. It was a small garden, just a narrow path that wound around two adjoining ponds, a perfectly useless footbridge spanning the narrow channel where the two ponds joined. Perhaps a child could cavort across that bridge, but it seemed largely there for show. The walls around the garden were too tall for anyone in the garden to see over, and the many prickly plants all around the base of the wall discouraged climbing.

There was just enough room for someone trapped indoors to take a quick turn, breathe a little fresher air, and then disappear back inside. Or at least that's what the three girls trapped inside did every day at exactly the same time.

Scout knew those girls. At least one of them would have balked at such a regimental schedule. But then Scout knew they weren't the ones deciding the schedule. They were prisoners in all but name.

Her friends. She and Daisy had spent weeks refining their plan to break them out, but the time wasn't right to make a move. Not yet.

The waiting was driving Scout mad.

But she came every day just to see them and make sure they were OK.

The twins emerged first from between the trees. Seeta was looking stronger than Scout had seen her in a long time, walking on her own, with her sister Geeta hovering near to catch her if she should stumble again.

The Months had been true to their word. Their doctors had gotten Seeta out of her coma, and she was recovering. Slowly, to be sure, but Scout supposed that was always going to be true.

She had come so very close to dying, her breathless body freezing as she tumbled through the vacuum of space. They had caught her, but not quite in time. That she was walking through a garden at all was a gift.

Then Emilie appeared, hands in her pockets and head down, as if looking at her own feet as she walked. Everything about her body language said this walk was mandatory, and she didn't like it even if she doubtlessly needed it. Scout couldn't help but smile. Emilie's restless longing to be back indoors was strong.

It also meant the Months were still letting her have access to their own library, as much as they had cut Emilie off from their cousin's library. Even filtered information was information Emilie could use. She was very good at inferring what was missing in what she saw. If anyone had worked out that Scout herself was also at Galactic Central, it was Emilie.

But none of the three ever looked up, ever tried to see beyond the walls of their prison. From their viewpoint, the other islands around them must have looked cold and remote, unfeelingly distant, with their relentless stone walls blocking the view. But Scout kept hoping at least Geeta would see her one of these days.

Not that she could recognize her from such a distance, not with unassisted vision, but Scout still hoped they knew she hadn't abandoned them.

After a few minutes of walking around the pond, Seeta pausing to toss crumbs of food over the water—to feed some fish she couldn't see, Scout assumed—they were called back indoors.

Scout blinked, and her glasses returned to normal settings. The day was colder than normal, her hands growing numb even inside her gloves. She gave a moment's consideration to not finishing her daily rounds, but quickly dismissed it.

She had to check. Nothing ever changed, but she still had to see.

She pulled off the gloves and stuffed them back in her pockets, blowing on her hands briefly before reaching up for the handholds.

She was only a dozen or so meters from the top of the wall, but everything above the ledge she had been resting on was much smoother, the handholds smaller and further apart. Her muscles still knew where they all were without looking, but she forced herself to take it slow, to be sure the stone wasn't slick under her fingertips before putting weight on it.

She didn't actually know what would happen if she fell. Daisy had said the cloud that enclosed the islands of Galactic Central was human made, a construct designed to contain atmosphere around the disparate islands that were in a lot of ways like separate city-states. They could move away from enemies, closer to allies, all without leaving the cloud.

The islands generated their own gravity. The wall she was scaling was nearly flush with the island, but not quite. There had been a narrow band of rock under her feet when she had stood at the bottom. If she fell further out than that band of rock, would she keep falling?

Daisy had said she'd have all of her falling momentum, but the direction could be random, depending on lots of things that didn't make a lot of sense to Scout just yet. She had been learning a lot of physics with her teaching AI Warrior, but they still hadn't covered more than the basics, hampered as they were with Scout's poor grasp of the math involved.

But if even Daisy didn't know where a falling person would end up—if they would drift lost in the cloud forever or plunge out of it into the vacuum of space—Scout knew it wasn't worth taking chances. Just assume a fall was as fatal here as anywhere else she had ever been.

She pulled herself up on the top of the wall, not technically wide enough to accommodate a person, but Scout was small enough to pull herself up into a half sit and look around.

Below her were rolling hills of waving grass, a shallow stream curving around to her left. Here and there, a black or brown dot moved, all but hidden in the grass. One of Bo's beloved horses.

She looked the whole scene over very carefully, but nothing had changed. She double-checked, but another blast of cold wind dissuaded her from checking for a third time.

Bo said he would get a message to her if he needed to speak with her. He hadn't said what form the message would take, just that it would be obvious. So why couldn't she get over the feeling that she was missing it?

Because it had been so long, Scout said to herself with a sigh as she climbed back down, past the ledge to the base of the wall itself. She and Daisy had been here for more than forty days, and still nothing had happened.

The Torreses were in protective custody, unable to ever leave the massive, towering court building that dominated one of the larger interior islands. Scout had seen not a hair of either of them, but Bo said they were safe. Safe, but far out of her reach, just like Geeta, Seeta, and Emilie.

The McGillicuddys had stayed on Schneeheim, and Bo promised her they were safe as well. But the one time he had communicated with her, back when she and Daisy had just arrived at Galactic Central in their stolen ship with all the best tech, including encrypted communication systems, he had only been able to give her the broadest strokes of the situation.

That and his promise to send her a message if anything changed. Surely they had the same idea of obvious, right?

Scout reached the rocky ground at the base of the wall and put her gloves on before reaching for the kite-like glider she had left carefully weighted down to keep it still while she climbed.

She blinked, and her glasses brightened briefly, letting her know they were prepared with anti-fogging measures should she need them. She kind of wished she had a pair of goggles to pull down over her eyes, just for the "I'm about to do this" ritual of it. Stepping off into nothingness was an act that should be marked, she thought.

She set the spine of the glider against her back, grasped the handles at the ends of the triangular wings in her gloved hands, and jumped out into the fog.

She spiraled down, but only for a moment. She felt a swell of wind beneath her and her body adjusted the glider to ride it, a movement she didn't even have to think about anymore. The wind carried her up, high over Bo Tajaki's island. She skirted well away from the Months' compound, just in case their security forces were on the lookout for her.

Then she folded her wings close to her sides and dove through layer after layer of cloud, angling down but also towards the center, to the heart of the city. She felt the heat on her cheeks as her glasses warmed up, not letting the droplets that wet her hair into slick clumps fog up her vision.

Then she felt a shiver run up her spine. She was surrounded by clouds, the wind whistling loudly past her ears. Why did she have the sudden feeling that she was about to be caught in the jaws of a trap?

Scout had learned the hard way to trust her instincts. Even though her rational mind was still insisting she was in the most sparsely populated quadrant of the cloud and no one would have any reason to be near her, she spread her wings, slowing her descent to a crawl, then leveling out when she reached the next patch of open sky between clouds.

She was just about to laugh at her own paranoia when five more gliders appeared, one by one. If they had been diving when she had, they had also pulled up when she had, matching her velocity even as they tightened their formation.

They were closing in around her, some a little lower and some a little higher, to maintain a sphere around her.

She had no idea who they were. But she knew trouble when she was in the middle of it. She had had far too much experience with it.

2

THE WIND GUSTED, snapping at the tight fabric of the glider wings against her back. Scout clutched the handles tightly as the wings wobbled back and forth. She'd gotten the hang of flying quickly, but that didn't change the fact that she'd only been doing it for a few days.

Watching the flyers surrounding her, it was obvious they had far more experience than she did. Flying with the gliders was a common teenage pursuit in Galactic Central, and judging by their size, it was teenagers flanking all around her.

Teenagers, or a bit younger.

The wind died down again, and the clouds closed in around them, the five other gliders disappearing in the fog around Scout. But she knew they were still there. The glasses on her cheeks heated up, quickly dispelling the droplets of moisture that were collecting in front of her eyes. She supposed the other kids had similar tech, but it was difficult to tell. In the brief glimpses she had gotten of them, they had seemed to be wearing all-black, tight-fitting clothes with hoods that covered their entire heads, nothing visible but their own reflective glasses built into their masks.

She'd seen other young people wearing something similar before.

But all white that time, to blend in with the snow that covered all of Schneeheim.

Black didn't blend in with anything, especially not in this softly pink sky. But maybe they weren't trying to hide anymore.

The clouds parted once more, and she saw they were still around her, but no closer than before. They were just flanking her as if waiting for something else to happen. She'd been heading back to the room she shared with Daisy and the dogs in the very center of the city of floating islands. They were nearly there. The islands here were much closer together, many even connected by delicate-looking bridges. The buildings were taller, some boxy like the buildings on *Amatheon Orbiter 1*, but others spiraling up like elongated snail shells or built like stacked platforms with no walls, just impossibly thin pillars holding the levels apart, like studies in maximizing negative space.

But everywhere she looked was swarming with people. Dense crowds had become normal for Scout. After years spending the bulk of her time alone in vast prairies, she never thought she would get used to people pressing in all around her, would be unbothered by it, but somehow she had.

More than that, at this very moment, those thronging crowds looked like the safest, most welcoming place to be.

Scout maintained her trajectory, trying to appear as if she didn't mind or even notice the five of them flying so close around her. Then she drew near one of the islands with the tall negative-space buildings. A providential updraft caught the wings of her glider, and she let it carry her up in the air, the others riding the same current with her. She sensed the air changing as the updraft died and flattened the wings close to her sides to dive back down to the island. She spread her wings at the last possible moment, shooting like a dart between the floors of one of the open buildings.

Floor probably wasn't the right word, she thought as she looked down at the plants growing everywhere below her. The different levels were like stacked gardens, but not pleasure gardens like the wealthier, more isolated islands had. These were vegetable patches with fruit orchards. She even saw a person at the edge of a field tending to a beehive. They looked up in surprise as she zipped past, losing altitude pretty steadily now that she was over an island with its artificial gravity pulling down on her.

She hadn't really thought she would evade her pursuers, and, indeed, they followed her with little trouble. Being more skilled flyers, they weren't losing altitude like Scout was. By the time she reached the end of the platform, the topmost branches of the trees were slapping at her, threatening to catch her and snatch her out of the air.

But then she was clear. She came out the other end, back out to the relatively weightless in-between place, and climbed on another current of air higher above the ever thicker clusters of islands.

Her pursuers flanked her once more, the two on either side of her almost ahead of her now. Still, they didn't move any closer. What were they waiting for?

Scout kept climbing up into the air until she could make out her destination. At the very heart of the cloud were the two largest islands, joined by a stone bridge. This bridge was the very opposite of delicate. It had its own artificial gravity and joined those two islands irrevocably.

It was also one of the most crowded places in Galactic Central. The marketplace.

She was never going to be able to outfly her pursuers, but on the ground, she might have a better chance.

She started to spiral down to land in the large square at the center of the market. She expected them to match her moves again, but this time the one on her left slid in closer to her, not quite close enough to catch hold of her, but more than enough to make Scout nervous. Then something flashed in their hand, but before Scout could quite see what it, it was tracing an arc through the air. Scout heard the hiss of a very sharp knife through the very thin fabric of her glider, and then she was falling.

One of the others tried to catch hold of her, to break her fall, but Scout dodged away from that extended hand.

The left wing of her glider was slashed in two, the tattered fabric flapping uselessly against her side. She extended her other arm, trying to catch as much air as she could. It wasn't enough to hold her weight, especially here directly over the market bridge. She was in full gravity here, not close enough to either edge of the enormous bridge to get back out into the floating place.

She grasped the wrist of her still-flying arm with her other hand as the buffets of wind pounded on the wing, threatening to tumble her over. She managed to stay level, to slow her fall, but it wasn't quite enough. The roofs looked like they were rushing up to meet her.

She angled her legs down, aiming for the top of the tallest steeply sloping roof. The moment her feet touched the tile, she threw off the remains of her now-useless glider.

Then she was sliding down the rooftop, still moving far too quickly down the tallest building on the bridge. There was still a lot more *down* for her to face without a gilder.

She tried to break her momentum with her heels and then her gloved hands, but the tiles were perfectly smooth. There wasn't so much as a gutter to catch hold of to keep her from vaulting off the end of the roof. Then she was once more flying through the air.

The building opposite had an awning over a dining area, just a decorative element, as there was not enough sunlight anywhere in Galactic Central to need any sort of shade. Nor rain either, so there was no reason to make the awning in any way sturdy. Scout's body punched right through it.

But she caught the very edge of it, where it wrapped around a support pole. It was enough to break her fall, but her weight started bending the cheap metal almost at once.

The last few weeks of rock-climbing had made her strong, but not strong enough to hang by her fingertips forever. She tried to pull herself higher, but she was already worn out from her climb up the wall. She watched in horror as her fingers pulled away from the pole one by one.

But when her grip gave way, she realized the ground was only a meter or so below her. When teaching her to rock climb, Daisy had also taught her how to fall. Scout didn't have time to think about it, just let the instinct from the practice take over. Her legs collapsed beneath her and she redirected her momentum into a tight forward roll.

Her whole body ached, but nothing was broken.

She got up and ran.

She didn't look behind her to see if her pursuers were still on her. She didn't need to. She could just feel them there, like their fixed gazes on her were little pinpricks.

Scout pushed her way through the thick crowd emerging from the island's transportation station, then slowed down so that she could just brush between them. Leaving a wake of angry people behind her was not going to help her escape.

Then she saw an opening between two of the shops and ran down the narrow alley into the next road that ran along the bridge.

She was getting closer to one of the sides, which was good, but there were probably three or four more lines of shops between her and the edge of the bridge.

And she no longer had her glider.

But she could deal with that when she got to the edge.

She reached another narrow alleyway that led to the next line of shops. She paused before running into it, just long enough to look back and see if her pursuers were still behind her.

They were. Their gliders were folded closed against their backs, but they still had them. They had the air of being willing to follow her forever, jogging with the unhurried gait of trained athletes.

Scout sprinted down the alleyway, then heard the sound of music. Mostly just the bass, a deep thumping that invited the people walking home from their workday to come inside and dance.

Scout plunged into the dark interior of the club, unzipping her jacket and unfurling her long blue scarf. She pulled a gray cap out of her pocket as she jogged down the ramp to the lower level of the club, slapping it on her head and tucking in the loose strands of her honey-colored hair.

Not much of a disguise—she doubted it would be enough—but if they stopped at the railing to scan the heads on the dance floor below, they might miss seeing her.

She had never gotten the hang of dancing, but one person simply plowing through all the dancing groups would be too noticeable. She watched the others around her and tried to mimic their movements, working her way across the floor, but not in an obvious way.

Even harder to do in a non-obvious way was watching for her

pursuers. She had to rely on that prickly feeling to tell her when they arrived.

She was halfway across the dance floor when she felt it. They were still with her.

But just in case they hadn't seen her yet, she maintained her dancing motion across the floor. There had to be a back door out of there. But she wasn't sure where to find it.

The lights pulsing with the driving beat would've been blinding if her glasses weren't automatically correcting for it. She focused on the dark corners, and they compensated for that as well.

She saw the outline of a doorway at the end of a short hall. She was nearly there.

But they were watching.

She danced closer to a group of girls about her age. They were catching each other's hands and spinning each other around, laughing at the almost-violence of it. Scout drew nearer and one of them caught her outstretched hand, pulling her into their group, spinning her and spinning her. Scout pretended to laugh and enjoy it. Then she grabbed one of the other girls, taking her own turn at spinning someone else before releasing her.

She had spun herself closer to the door. As unnoticeably as she could, she danced away from the group and blended back in with the crowd.

As she approached the short hallway that led to the back exit, she risked a look up at the banister. Two of her pursuers were there, easy to spot, even in their all-black clothing, as they were still wearing their hoods with reflective lenses over their eyes. There was no sign of the other three, but Scout knew if they had blended in with the crowd around her, they could be within arm's reach and she wouldn't be able to see them.

She turned and ran down the short hallway, throwing her weight against the heavy door to bang it open and then running up the steep steps that brought her back up to the street level of the bridge.

She was in another narrow alleyway. She ran to the left, quickly reaching the very edge of the bridge. The walls of the buildings on either side of her were flush against the balustrade.

There was no way out, no space to squeeze through to reach the next alley. She'd gone the wrong way.

She turned to run back the direction she'd come, but the door banged open once more and two of her pursuers spilled out, only taking a moment before catching sight of her standing against the bridge railing with the bright pink sky behind her. Then a third came out. This one tapped them each on the arm, and at that signal, all three of them started advancing on her.

Scout looked over her shoulder at the bridge railing. Normally she'd just vault over it, but normally she would have her glider with her. Without it, getting home was going to be a bit more complicated.

She backed up until the top of the balustrade pressed against the small of her back. The three of them were still advancing, but slowly. Their hands were up in a ready position, but no weapons visible. If one of these three was the one that had slashed the wing of her glider, there was no sign of a knife now.

But Scout wasn't anxious to see what they intended to do when they reached her. She hopped up on top of the balustrade, then got to her feet. The balustrade was too narrow for both of her feet at once, but she could put one foot in front of the other.

It got a bit trickier when she reached the building. She had to turn her body to walk with her back to the wall, the drop into nothingness before her.

Scout shut her eyes and swallowed hard, but her head was clear. The bouncing, tumbling-forward, off-balance feeling had been plaguing her less and less since she and Daisy had reached Galactic Central, but she still had episodes.

To her immense relief, she wasn't having one now. She opened her eyes and continued along the balustrade. She glanced back over her shoulder to see her three pursuers watching her, the reflective lenses under their black hoods making their intentions inscrutable.

Then one hopped up onto the balustrade to follow her. Scout turned her attention back to where she was going, hurrying her steps as much as possible.

She didn't hop down when she reached the next alley. She could see the island ahead of her, its barren, rocky foundation extending below the bridge. It jutted out into the void beneath the bridge. Not far, but perhaps far enough.

Her pursuers certainly wouldn't expect her to go this way.

Scout clutched the ends of her unzipped jacket, holding them out like the wings of a glider as much as she could. Then she ran along the balustrade, across the length of the alley, and then alongside the next building, butting up against it.

She stumbled, caught herself, and ran some meters more before stumbling again. This stumble she just went with it, pushing away from the bridge, letting herself tumble into the free fall zone. She only needed a little luck, to catch a gust to throw her back where she needed to be.

She had forgotten that while her glider was gone, her pursuers still had theirs.

And they were very skilled fliers.

3

THE AIR away from the bridge was bone-chillingly cold. Just like the air she had spent the whole afternoon in, but just a few moments running through the warmer air of the marketplace with its crush of people, and especially of the club packed with sweaty dancers, had been enough for her to acclimate to that more human temperature.

Now she was back out in the chill fog, and it sucked the breath out of her body. She gasped, drawing in a deep lungful. Her throat felt like it was frosting over, but the chill made its way to her brain, forcing her thoughts to run faster.

She needed that clarity badly. Her jump away from the bridge had taken her too far out into the nothingness but not enough forward towards the floating island, and the gust of air she had bet her life on wasn't there.

Plus, her jacket was not behaving as a glider nearly as well as she had hoped. She was shooting out, away from bridge and island both. Who knew where she would stop, but nothing she did with her jacket was changing her trajectory at all.

At last, she let go of it entirely, letting it flutter behind her as she reached underneath it to one of the many pouches on her belt. In a flash, she had a little gun in her hand. Not the pistol that had come with the belt—that was long since lost—but a smaller instrument with a different purpose.

She rolled over mid fall, firing back up at the bridge above her. The gun gave a soft pop, and a metallic dart shot up to the bridge, dragging coils of a cable so thin it was all but invisible in the sky. She quickly lost sight of it, but that didn't matter. She had just managed to fasten the other end of the cable to her belt before the dart struck home.

Her journey through the layers of clouds ended with a lurch and then she was swinging from the bottom of the bridge.

Back towards the gravity field.

At last, she had a chance to look around to spot her pursuers. The three who had been in the alley with her had dove out after her, but they had missed her sudden lurching stop. Scout tipped her head back as she swung to watch them spin their gliders around and circle back as they realized they had lost her.

She could see the other two at the edge of the bridge, looking over the balustrade. Then one of them pointed at her.

She didn't have much time. She toyed with the idea of working her way along the cable to the bottom of the bridge, but the more time she took to get where she was going, the more likely it was that they would follow her there. For all sorts of reasons, that place had to stay a secret.

So instead, she waited until her lazy arc reentered the gravity field. She dropped to the very end of the cable with another lurch, but she was prepared for that and quickly started swinging her body weight.

It was maddeningly slow at first, and although the clouds around the bridge were thickening, she could still catch glimpses of her pursuers in black. Which meant they could catch glimpses of her.

She swung harder, really picking up momentum. She whistled through the air, her jacket flaring out behind her. Then she arced out wide, beyond the range of the bridge's gravity field, to hang motionless at the end of the rope for just a moment before zipping back the way she'd come. But not a straight line; a wide arc that carried her into the darkness between the bottom of the bridge and the very edge of the island. The glasses in front of her eyes quickly adjusted to the lower light, and she watched as the massive stone blocks of the bridge bottom drew ever closer. She was aiming for a point as close to the far side of the bridge as possible. If they lost sight of her, they might think she had swung clear around it, had leaped up and over the opposite balustrade.

At least, that was her plan.

She realized the moment she was free from the cable and was sailing through the last bit of open air, hands outstretched to catch the boulders of the island's exposed bedrock, that she might have overestimated her momentum. She didn't land on the ledge she had been aiming for. The gravity field was dragging her down too fast for that.

For a horrible moment, she thought she was going to miss the island entirely. Then her fingertips brushed rock, and she seized it, gritting her teeth as the weight of her body tried to drag her down from her handholds.

Once more, she found herself dangling from her fingertips, but this time with her feet kicking over nothingness. Although she was at the island's lowest point, the artificial gravity was still pulling her down. Or maybe pushing her down from above, where the mass of the island was? She wasn't exactly sure how it worked.

With a great amount of effort, she managed to get first her left elbow and then everything up to her left shoulder over the lip of the boulder. But she couldn't hang there forever, legs still dangling uselessly, no matter how exhausted she was. With another loud grunt, she got her right arm up, and she leaned forward and pulled her chest and then her stomach over the cold, slick edge of the boulder.

Then she just collapsed, lying flat on the top of the boulder with the bulk of her legs still hanging over the edge, waiting for the muscles in her arms to stop twitching.

She heard a murmur of voices, and she lifted just her head to look past her feet and out from under the bridge to where her five pursuers were describing lazy circles through the sky on both sides of the bridge. Clearly a search pattern.

Scout pulled her legs up, got her knees under her, and scrambled back from the edge of the boulder as far as she could. Then she climbed over the next boulder, crawling deeper into the impenetrable darkness between the slope of the island's exposed bedrock and the bottom of the stone bridge.

She didn't know if the lenses she could see under their hoods were like her glasses or not. Probably best to assume they were. The darkness wasn't going to protect her. And their search pattern was drawing closer.

She found handholds and began the steady climb across the mountain of boulders to the very center under the bridge. The bridge hadn't gotten any smaller, and the climb was exhausting, but she didn't dare take breaks.

At last, she reached her goal: a deep fissure between two of the largest boulders. She turned sideways, pushing one shoulder into the narrow gap, then paused to get a visual on each of her pursuers. She had to be sure they weren't looking her way.

They were all under the bridge now, three on one side and two on the other, slowly making their way from under the balustrades to the center. None of them saw her, but that was going to change quickly if she didn't get out of sight.

Scout sucked in her breath, then squeezed between the rocky protuberance that dug into the front of her neck just above her collarbones and the other that dug into the small of her back. It was like being choked and stabbed in the kidneys at the same time. Not pleasant, but she'd done this before. She knew exactly how to contort her body to slip through into the larger space beyond.

It was completely dark on the far side, her own body largely blocking the little light that made its way in through the fissure from the less-than-total darkness under the bridge. But darkness was no problem for her glasses, and even without them, she had come this way so many times her feet knew exactly where to step.

The fissure ran for only a few meters, took a sudden turn to the left and another back to the right, and then ceased to resemble a natural formation in the rock, if indeed it even was. Scout had her doubts.

Now she was in a long hallway lit with little red lights, not enough to penetrate the darkness at the cave mouth, but enough for even those without glasses like hers to see enough to make their way to whichever of the endless rows of doors they called home.

None of the doors were marked, and they were all locked. Scout had occasionally seen one of her neighbors moving through this hallway, but had never made eye contact with any of them. They were all teens like her and Daisy, living here in the sublevel of the largest of the floating islands, down beneath even the level of the sewage treatment facilities. They all had reasons for living in hiding and no interest in sharing those reasons with each other.

It had been the perfect place for Daisy to bring Scout after selling the ship they had arrived on. Scout didn't know how Daisy had even known about it, and Daisy wouldn't talk about the things she had done those first days in Galactic Central, just like she didn't talk about what she did all day now.

Travel through hyperspace on that super-fast ship had been bad for Scout. She had been so very sick, not just during the journey but for a long, long time after. When the ship had arrived at Galactic Central, Scout had been too sick to move; she knew that much.

She knew she had talked to Bo, but only because Daisy had told her so. She couldn't even summon a mental picture that felt real, and not like a daydream in which she inserted everything Daisy said Bo had told her.

Her memories were little more than flashes of images, snapshots that she didn't think her mind even had in chronological order. But someone had helped Daisy bring Scout down here to the largest of the islands, to bring her all the way down to the sublevels deep within the bedrock, to one of these little rooms that must once have been intended for storage but had long since been forgotten by those who lived in the city above.

But the teens knew they were here. And one of them had told Daisy. And now it was home.

Scout stopped at the fifteenth door on her left and took a moment to push back her still-wet hair, adjust her twisted clothing, and take a deep breath before typing the code into the pad on the wall next to the door.

The lock gave a little click that was all but lost in the sound of enthusiastic barking from the room behind. The more persistent was a high-pitched bark only a degree or two away from being a yip. The other, more considered bark was deeper, almost frightening, even when it was clearly a bark of welcome.

Scout's face broke out into a broad smile even before she opened the door just enough to slip inside without letting anything get out past her.

It was a damp, dark, miserable place to live, far from fresh air or light or warmth. But her dogs were in it.

And that made it home.

4

WHEN SCOUT HAD BEEN Bo Tajaki's personal guest on his starship, she had been given her own room with a walled-in garden, the bedroom and living room both full of light from the artificial sun, the kitchen stocked with delicious food, and the bathroom equipped with the most wondrous shower she had ever had the pleasure of cleaning up in.

On Schneeheim, she had been given a cabin of her own, small but snug against the cold wind. The bed had been a mountain of warmth, layer after layer of soft blankets for her and the dogs to nest in.

She had gotten to spend exactly one night in each of those places. But this place, this cold, damp space with barely enough room for the bed on the floor and the table and two chairs beside it—this place she had been sleeping in for weeks now.

But she didn't mind it. She had never grown up with the sort of luxury Bo Tajaki took for granted. She preferred the dry, hot air of her prairie home, but she didn't mind sleeping in this place.

She knew for certain it came with no strings attached.

Scout slipped quickly inside the room, shutting the door behind her before either of the dogs could escape.

Not that they were interested in getting past her. No, they were both beside themselves with joy, just as they were every day at this time when she came back home.

Scout dropped to one knee, tucking Shadow's little rat terrier body close to her side and reaching out to the frantically wiggling Gert. Gert leaned her head into Scout's ear scratches and gave a contented sigh.

Once they both seemed content with the amount of attention she had given them, she got back to her feet and turned on the little heater built into one of the walls. She and Daisy didn't run it when they were out, as the fuel cells were expensive, but the dogs didn't mind the cold. They just burrowed under the bedcovers.

The little light standing on the middle of the table she did leave on for them, though. The idea of her dogs waiting for her return in the dark was too much.

Daisy hadn't objected. Scout didn't know exactly what Daisy did during the day, only that every night she returned with hot food and occasionally an extra coin or two for fuel cells, clothes, or other needs. So far, they hadn't had to dip into the money she had gotten for selling the starship they had arrived on.

That money might prove very necessary when Shi Jian finally showed up. The two of them might have to flee or find another place to hide, one not so cheap.

Those kids. Had they worked for Shi Jian? The child assassins that had pursued her in the past had been a lot wilier than those five, and yet if they didn't work for Shi Jian, who were they?

"Hello, Teacher," Scout said as she sat down at the table.

The AI hologram who was her tutor appeared in the chair opposite. "Hello, Scout," she said. "You look worried."

"Preoccupied," Scout agreed. "You can access Bo Tajaki's library from here, right?"

"Correct," Warrior said. "Do you need to do some research?"

"Not exactly," Scout said. "Maybe more searching news reports or something. I was chased today by a group of five people. I think they were my age; they were all using gliders. They dressed all in black with masks over their faces. They had reflective lenses over their eyes, but they didn't seem to have any sort of enhanced vision."

"How could you tell?" Warrior asked.

"I hid from them in the dark," Scout said. "I would have spotted myself easily, but they didn't."

"Interesting," Warrior said. "Perhaps the lenses were just to protect their eyes from the elements?"

"Maybe," Scout conceded. "Can you dig into it?"

But before Warrior could answer, the door beeped and then swung open. The dogs barked their greetings as Daisy fumbled through the doorway, arms loaded with packages.

Scout didn't have to tell Warrior to disappear. She never had to. The AI just knew without Scout ever saying it out loud that she was to be kept secret.

It was almost creepy how she seemed to read Scout's mind. Creepy, but convenient.

Scout scrambled up from her chair to help Daisy get in the door. That mainly involved restraining the dogs until the door was closed and she had dumped the packages on the table and collapsed into the chair.

"Long day?" Scout asked, but when Daisy looked up at her, it was with assessing eyes.

"What happened?" she asked.

Scout touched her fingertips to her cheeks. She hadn't been hurt, so what was Daisy seeing?

"I got chased by some troublemakers," she said dismissively. "I gave them the slip in the marketplace. They didn't follow me back here."

"Shi Jian?" Daisy asked.

"No, definitely not," Scout said.

"You're sure?"

"Positive," Scout said.

But Daisy was still looking her over with a little worried line between her brows. "Are you still feeling OK? No episodes?"

"No episodes," Scout said.

The tumbling, falling, bobbing, spinning feeling that had made her completely unable to function while traveling on the high-speed starship had not gone away when they had dropped back to normal speed. It hadn't gone away even when they had left the ship. It had taken days and days before Scout was even able to sit up, let alone move about. And even then, she would occasionally feel it recur. But not lately.

Scout wished she could trust that it was gone for good, but she kept waking up uncertain if it was back. She would lie still for several minutes, unwilling to move her body until she was sure her mind was not going to freak out and think a lot more motion was going on than there was the moment she sat up.

It was a deeply unpleasant feeling.

Finally, Daisy looked away, turning her attention to the packages on the table. "We should eat while it's still hot," Daisy said.

"It smells good," Scout said, grateful for the change in conversation. "That spicy chicken thing again?"

"Different spicy chicken thing," Daisy said with a small smile. "I'm not sure what the sauce is, but it's green instead of red. Try it."

Scout popped the lid off the container and dug a spoon into the soupy liquid. There was a variety of vegetables in there as well as the bits of chicken. As usual, nothing that Scout could identify. Food from all over the galaxy was available in Galactic Central; some things were similar to food they had on Amatheon, but others were completely alien to her.

Daisy watched her face as she put the spoonful in her mouth. Scout's first thought was that it wasn't as spicy as it smelled, but as she chewed, the spiciness kept building. By the time she swallowed, the entire interior of her mouth was buzzing warmly.

Scout could feel the broad smile on her face, and Daisy smiled back. "I've never met anyone who adores spicy food the way you do," she said, lifting the lid from her own container. She'd given herself a smaller serving, either to be social or just for the taste. She met her own need for sustenance in quite a different way.

"Did you find another supplier for what you need?" Scout asked. Now she was the one looking assessingly at her friend. Did Daisy look pale? It was hard to tell in the artificial light. And although Daisy was keeping her hair cut short on the back and sides, she had let the front grow long enough to cover her eyes when she bent her head. Like she was doing now.

"Yes, I did," Daisy said. "It's a different manufacturer than what I've consumed before, but it seems to be working just fine. I haven't felt this alert in weeks."

"That's good," Scout said.

"How are your friends doing?" Daisy asked between spoonfuls.

"Good, good," Scout said. "Seeta is looking stronger by the day. I wish I could find a way to communicate with them, though. Maybe a system of signals, like we have with Bo."

"We would have to get a message to them first," Daisy said. "If you want to risk it—"

"No," Scout said. She and Daisy had mapped out the Months' entire island. They had found a way in through the drainage system that ran under the garden pond. They had refined their plan for getting in and getting her three friends out.

But it would likely only work once. She couldn't risk exposing the route to the Months' security team just to see her friends, to talk to them.

"Any word from Bo?" Daisy asked.

"Not yet," Scout sighed. "Any news on the street?"

"Of a gossipy sort," Daisy said with a shrug. "The Tajaki trade dynasty has been a ripe subject for works of fiction for centuries. The blow-by-blow of two members of the dynasty engaged in a legal feud is pretty much all anyone in the public houses talk about. But I haven't heard anything relevant or interesting. And no mention of a woman in black lurking about anywhere."

"Where *is* she?" Scout asked, not remotely for the first time.

Daisy shrugged, scraping at the bottom of her bowl for the last bit of spicy broth. "Sooner or later, she'll be here. There's nothing we can do but wait."

Scout sighed. She hated waiting. How long did it take to regrow an arm, anyway?

Or would she regrow it? Perhaps she just needed to replace it, like you would on a robot. Or perhaps it was both: replace her metal skeleton and then regrow the enhanced flesh over it.

She could have asked Daisy, but didn't. Daisy didn't like to talk about her own enhancements. Scout didn't blame her. She had not been given any choice in the matter, and the endless surgeries had been extremely painful. Her entire childhood had been one agonizing procedure after another, with endless training between.

All to make her the perfect assassin, easy to underestimate with her teenaged body.

And she hadn't been the youngest of Shi Jian's assassins. Not by a long shot.

Daisy stacked the bowls and lids together to carry them out to the water spigot at the end of the hall they shared with all their neighbors.

Then Scout saw a flashing light in the corner of her eye. She realized when Daisy didn't react to it, that it wasn't in the room. It was coming from her glasses.

"I'll take those," Scout said, grabbing for the dishes.

"Are you sure?" Daisy asked.

"Yeah, you've been working all day," Scout said.

"You've been scaling walls," Daisy said.

"The dogs need a walk too," Scout said.

Daisy shrugged, and Scout pulled the dogs' leashes from one of the pouches on her belt. She clipped them to the dogs' collars but didn't bother holding the other end as she opened the door and let them out. She could snatch them up if they encountered anyone in the hallway, but they almost never did.

The dogs ran out of the room, tearing around the corner at the end of the hall and disappearing in the direction of the spigot. There was a deeper cavern beyond, more of a natural rock formation like the fissure, enormous with a sandy floor. She let the dogs do their business there. She felt a little guilty she hadn't taken them out the minute she'd gotten home. Being chased had clearly distracted her.

"Hello, Teacher," she said as soon as she had rounded the corner.

"Hello, Scout," Warrior said, appearing mid step beside her.

"That was you blinking the light?"

"Yes, I hoped you'd infer that," Warrior said. "I have news about your pursuers."

"Shi Jian?" Scout asked.

"No," Warrior said. "They are a youth group that does not appear to answer to any adult figure. They're new on the scene, only showing up shortly after you arrived. Reports are scant, since they don't seem to be committing any crimes beyond 'lurking.'"

"Lurking is a crime?" Scout asked.

"Some people like to think so," Warrior said. "But the security forces in Galactic Central don't consider it one. They will note the time and place in case it should be linked to an actual crime later. The kids in black lurk on rooftops and always escape on gliders when approached."

"And they don't answer to an adult," Scout said. "So, what are they up to?"

"They do report to another adolescent," Warrior told her. "Here, I'll show you an image on your glasses."

Scout stopped walking as her vision was suddenly dominated by the image of the marketplace at midday. The image expanded, growing blurry as it zoomed in on a girl in an oversized red hoodie talking to three kids in black clothes. The girl turned and left them, fading into the crowds around the vegetable market. But just before she faded from view, she looked back over her shoulder, giving Scout a good look at her face.

"That's Sparrow!" Scout said, recognizing the girl she had met on the Months' starship just before she had left her home world behind. "She's still with the Months?"

"Perhaps," Warrior said. "Or perhaps she came this far, then left their employ."

"I should stake out the Months' island closer to the arrival gate," Scout said. "See if I can spot her."

"I think that would be wise, yes," Warrior said.

Scout washed the bowls and lids, then whistled for the dogs to rejoin her. They came barreling up the sloping corridor, tongues lolling and eyes bright. They walked beside Scout all the way back to the room.

When they got inside, Scout saw that Daisy had already gone to bed. She needed little sleep, but Scout suspected she liked to lie down and close her eyes just to have some time alone in her own head.

Scout didn't know what Daisy did all day, only that it involved visiting a public house and resulted in small amounts of cash. And that Daisy didn't want to talk about it.

It seemed to be taking a toll.

Scout got the dogs settled, then turned out the light. She could wait until she knew more before saying anything to Daisy.

But if she could get to Sparrow, she might learn what had happened to Shi Jian.

She was about to drift off to sleep when one last worrying thought crossed her mind.

Why was Sparrow using these kids to get to Scout? To help her, or to harm her?

5

DAISY WAS UP EARLY the next morning. The dogs snuggled closer to Scout's warmth, but she hitched herself up on one elbow, rubbing the sleep from her eyes.

"Daisy?" she said.

"Sorry, didn't mean to wake you," Daisy said in little more than a whisper. "You can go back to sleep. I need to head out early today. Lots to do."

"I wanted to ask you something," Scout said.

Daisy didn't respond right away. But then she switched the table lamp on to its lowest setting and turned to look at Scout. There was a guarded expression on her face, and Scout guessed she was bracing herself for Scout to ask prying questions about what she did all day.

Not that she didn't wonder every day what her friend was up to. But, having secrets of her own, Scout respected that Daisy would tell her everything she needed to know when it was important and the rest when she was ready.

"Do you know another way out of this place besides the fissure under the bridge?" Scout asked as she sat up. Shadow made a soft, protesting sound and burrowed deeper under the blanket. Gert didn't stir at all.

"Another way out?" Daisy repeated. She looked around the room and then back at Scout. "Where's your glider?"

"Yeah, I lost that," Scout said.

"Ugh, I'm just too distracted these days," Daisy said, rubbing tiredly at her face. "You said there were troublemakers. I didn't follow up on that."

"It's not serious," Scout said. "Just a bunch of kids our age or a little younger. No enhancements or anything, just normal kids."

"How did you lose the glider?" Daisy persisted.

"So, okay, one of them slashed the wing with a knife, but they were just trying to force me down. If they had wanted me dead, they could have done worse."

"What *did* they want?" Daisy asked.

"I'm working on that," Scout said. "But on my terms. I would rather not run into them again if I can help it. I can plot a different course out to the Tajaki island; that's not a problem. But I will need a new glider, and a different way out of here would help too."

"I got our gliders from a kid at the end of the hall," Daisy said. "I hope he's an early riser, or I might have to spend a little extra for waking him."

"Sorry, I should have mentioned about the glider last night," Scout said.

"Maybe you should stay in today anyway," Daisy said.

"No, I can't," Scout said.

"Your friends will be fine without you checking on them for one day," Daisy said.

"It's not that," Scout said. "What if Bo Tajaki leaves me a message? I have to check every day. I have to be sure."

"I can check," Daisy said. "Although you'd have to tell me what I'm looking for."

"I can't," Scout said. "I don't know what it will be. You said that he said I would know it when I saw it. I'm not sure if that means it will be something specifically targeted at me or something anyone could puzzle out."

"Shi Jian keeps bouncing from wanting to kill us to wanting to take us alive and recruit us. Are you sure these troublemakers weren't part of her army?"

"They definitely didn't have enhancements," Scout said. "I slipped away by hiding in the shadows under the bridge. They were right there, circling around in a search formation, but they never saw me."

"It could be a ruse," Daisy said, unconvinced.

"I'm working a lead," Scout said. "I think I know who they report to; I just don't know what they wanted with me."

"Who do you think they report to?" Daisy asked.

"Sparrow, the Space Farer girl who was in the Months' court of pirates," Scout said. "I've seen video of her. I know she came here with them. I'm not sure if she's still with them, or if she's on her own, or what she wants from me."

"Okay," Daisy said slowly. "I can ask around, too. I'm guessing we're thinking along the same lines: confront her directly when you can find her, but in the meantime, stay away from these troublemaker kids."

"Exactly," Scout agreed.

"I'll figure out what I can," Daisy said. "I know some people I can ask first. But Scout, promise me you won't confront anyone alone. If you find out where she is, come get me."

"Come get you from where?" Scout asked. She held her breath, half certain that Daisy would abandon the beginnings of their plan for the sake of keeping her whereabouts secret.

But then she straightened her spine and looked Scout right in the eye. "There's a large public house at the far end of the bridge. The only way off the bridge to that island is a series of archways through the public house itself; you can't miss it. If you don't see me there, ask for Ruby."

"Who's Ruby?" Scout asked, but when Daisy's face flushed, she held up her hands as if to snatch that question back. "Ask for Ruby, got it."

Daisy slipped out the door, and Scout got out of bed and washed in the bucket of water they kept at the head of the bed. The water was so cold she expected to see ice forming over the surface, but the sting of it chased the last of the sleepiness from her mind.

Daisy came back with a pink glider, an exact match to the one she had lost. Except for the color. Scout preferred earth tones. At the moment, she only cared about being able to stay aloft.

"He said there are a bunch of ways out of here," Daisy said. "Follow any of the hallways; none of them dead-end. Some lead up to the street above, some just to the sewer levels. But the largest opening is at the far end of the cave. It leads to a fissure on the other side of the island."

Scout nodded as she pulled on her boots.

"Scout, these places are well known to the locals," Daisy said. "Any of them could already be staked out for an ambush. Or all of them."

"I'll be careful," Scout said. "Honestly, I don't know why they didn't just try talking to me, but I'm certain they weren't trying to really hurt me. I don't think Sparrow is my enemy."

"A lot could have changed since you saw her last," Daisy said.

"I know," Scout said, getting to her feet. "I'll be extra careful. And I won't confront her without you there. Although she's just an ordinary kid. Not even twelve."

"She's got others to do her bidding," Daisy said. "That's power."

"I'll check Bo's compound for a message, then I fly straight back here," Scout promised. "The dogs are due for a full day's romp with me, anyway."

"Okay," Daisy said. "I'll see you at dinner."

"Stay safe," Scout said.

Daisy nodded absentmindedly, then disappeared out the door.

Ruby?

Scout gave herself a little shake. It didn't matter. It wasn't her business.

And yet she couldn't help wondering again what Daisy did all day.

Scout brought the dogs down to the cave and let them run about for a bit until she had identified the tunnel the glider-maker had told Daisy about. Then she brought them back up to the room, ignoring their doggy protests as she shut them up inside the small, boring space with the wash bucket of water and a few handfuls of kibble strewn in various hideaways for them to find. She had to leave them with something to keep them occupied, poor things. They were used to a far more active and interesting life.

Then she carried her new glider through the cave, down the long, unlit tunnel that passed under the city above. It took nearly an hour to reach the far side.

This place was actually nicer for takeoffs than the fissure under the bridge. There, she had to jump and unfurl her wings as she fell. It had been absolutely terrifying the first few times.

But the tunnel opened out on a ledge covered with sand like the cave below. There was plenty of room not only to unfurl her glider wings but to get a running start, to hit the air with a good amount of forward momentum. She dropped only a meter or two before catching a blast of current that carried her spiraling high over the island city.

Although the skies over the city were full of other kids on gliders riding the winds, none of them appeared to be wearing black. Certainly, none of them were closing in on her or even looking her way.

Scout spread her wings and soared through the misty clouds toward the familiar far-off district where both sets of Tajaki cousins had their estates. Scout knew Bo shared his compound with a few distant members of his family, but she had never met them or even known their names. She only knew they were the reason she couldn't just walk in the door and talk to Bo directly. They were the reason she had to watch for subtle clues to be sure she wasn't missing a message.

Although Daisy had told her the weather here never really changed, the air felt warmer than it had the day before. Perhaps she was just plunging through fewer clouds.

She reached the base of the wall of the Tajaki island compound and carefully stashed her glider behind an outcropping of rock where it wouldn't get damaged or blown away. Then she started the long climb back up to the narrow ledge.

It was early, too early for Seeta, Geeta, and Emilie to be out in the garden, but she paused there anyway. She zoomed her glasses in on every detail of the place, staring down into every open garden, trying to peer through every window and door.

The windows all flashed brightly back at her as if reflecting intense sunlight back at her. And yet, as always, Galactic Central was all the pink, cloudy softness of a foggy morning, no proper sun anywhere.

She suspected this was some sort of anti-spying technology. If

Sparrow were anywhere inside that building, Scout was not going to determine that just by looking through the windows.

Nothing had changed in the little garden around the pond. She wished again that there was a way to get them a message, to at least let them know she was there and was watching over them, but there wasn't.

At last, Scout scaled the last of the wall, pulling herself up on the narrower top to look down on the grasslands below.

Scores of horses were grazing closer to her than she had ever seen them before. They usually didn't cross the little river that ran parallel to the outer wall. She had taken it for granted that the river was a barrier, that she would never see them so close.

Was this the message?

If so, what did it mean?

"Hello, Teacher," Scout said.

"Hello, Scout," Warrior said, appearing in front of her, straddling the wall and looking down at the grasslands just as Scout was. "Interesting."

"It's the message?" Scout said.

"Don't you see it?" Warrior asked. "Adjust your glasses to read heat."

Scout didn't have to; the glasses heard Warrior's words as a command and adjusted themselves.

The bodies of the horses glowed a warm shade of red, but several of them had something more going on. It looked like someone had painted their skin with… cold. How was that possible?

"Does it hurt them?" Scout asked.

"No, it's likely just a surface layer of nanites repelling heat. They don't feel a thing," Warrior said.

Scout looked from horse to horse. The cold patterns against their warm bodies were forming letters, but the letters made no sense.

"It doesn't spell anything," Scout said.

"He must have been pressed for time," Warrior said. "Otherwise, he could have trained them to stay in formation. You'll have to work it out from what you have."

Scout frowned. Her AI already knew the answer, but because it was a teacher first, it wouldn't just tell her.

Scout looked at the letters again. There were only five, although some of them repeated. Was that part of the word or part of Bo's effort to be sure she had all the information, even if some of the horses wandered off to other parts of the enclosure?

"Court?" Scout said at last. "The courthouse. He wants me to go to the courthouse."

"Very good," Warrior said.

"Do you have any idea why? Any news?" Scout asked.

"Nothing in the feeds," Warrior said. "But he's in a position to know things before that knowledge goes public."

Scout bit her lip. "I have to get to Daisy."

"I think that's wise," Warrior agreed. "And may I express again my assessment that she is a friend worthy of all of your trust?"

"Yes," Scout said, "you've said."

"And yet my existence remains a secret."

"Goodbye, Teacher," Scout said, then started the climb back down to her glider.

She knew she could trust Daisy. Daisy had saved her life more than once.

She knew she should trust Daisy. Daisy had forgiven her for killing her little sister, Clementine. Granted, Clementine had been shaped into a monster by Shi Jian, and Scout had only done it because Clementine had been about to kill Gert, but still. Forgiveness for that had been beyond Scout's hopes.

She had no reason not to trust Daisy, and she knew that. What she didn't know was why she couldn't just tell Daisy that she had a teaching AI. Especially as she was more than half convinced that Daisy, who had been spying on Shi Jian while hiding inside the walls of Bo Tajaki's starship, already knew that Bo had gifted it to Scout. He had consulted with Shi Jian about nearly everything; they must have discussed it.

But she couldn't bring herself to say anything about it out loud, or even just to summon Warrior when Daisy was around. Was she a glutton for the guilty feelings of keeping a secret from her closest friend?

Or had so many years living alone with her dogs made her physically incapable of trusting another human?

She didn't like that thought. It made her sound broken. Not fixable. And she didn't think that was true.

And yet, Warrior remained a secret.

Scout dropped the last couple of meters to the rocky ledge, then deployed her glider and leaped out into the sky.

She and Daisy had to get to the courthouse right away. Everything else would wait.

6

SCOUT KNEW EXACTLY where to find the public house Daisy had described. She had flown over it many times. It was larger than any other single building in the marketplace, providing a transition from the smaller shops and restaurants to the larger government buildings on the island itself.

Scout spiraled down to land in the middle of the street on the bridge in front of the house. People were streaming past her in both directions, towards the markets behind her and towards the open plaza beyond the public house. She could just see the steps that led up to the massive court building on the far side of the tiered fountain that dominated the plaza.

Scout gave her glider a swift jerk, and it collapsed back to its storage configuration, wings folded against the central spine so tightly it resembled little more than a tallish walking stick.

The public house had no doors, just open doorways that revealed little of the dark interior. But she could hear the sounds of people talking and laughing and carousing in a manner that felt incongruous with the early hour.

She could also smell the odors of people carousing. The sour smell of spilled beer left too long on the stone floor, the juicy aroma of meat grilling over an open flame, the richer scent of browning butter.

What were they cooking with browned butter? Scout's stomach was growling at her loudly, reminding her she had left in too much of a hurry to grab anything for breakfast.

But she was still in a hurry. She grasped her glider/stick and plunged into the dark interior of the public house.

It was bigger on the inside. The ceiling was lost in shadows far above her—she had expected that—but there were also sublevels dug down into the stone of the bridge itself. Every dimly lit table seemed to float on its own platform, letting the proprietor truly maximize all dimensions of the space to cram customers in.

And that space was crammed full. Scout didn't even know where to start looking for Daisy. Or Ruby, as she was called here. She took a few hesitant steps further inside.

A flash of red caught the corner of her eye, but when she turned to follow it, she saw nothing but drab clothing made even dingier by the inadequate light.

Scout rose up on tiptoe, then ducked down to try that angle between the platforms that insisted on bobbing ever so gently up and down. She was certain it was Sparrow's red hoodie that she had seen, but there was no sign of it now.

"A bit of a rough crowd for you, I'm guessing," someone said. Scout straightened, gripping her glider tightly in both hands across her body, but the youth talking to her didn't have a threatening look to him. Not with his hands thrust deep within his pockets. But there was no mistaking the strength in his bare arms, and the tattoo of a dragon coiling around his arm with its tail wrapped around his wrist and its eyes glaring balefully at her from over his shoulder had a sinister look to it. "It's mostly ship crews here, looking to blow off some steam. Maybe not your crowd."

"I'm looking for Ruby," Scout said, and the youth's eyebrows rose.

"A friend of Ruby," he said, looking her over as if she would have some identifying mark to prove she was.

"Is she here? It's urgent," Scout said.

"She's just over there," he said, pointing to a doorway to Scout's left, one that opened out onto one of the archways that led from bridge to plaza. "Probably give her a minute, though."

At first, Scout could only see the silhouette of two bodies moving against the brighter light from the doorway. Then her glasses adapted and she could see the details. Daisy, wearing the same tight pants and sleeveless shirt as the youth standing beside Scout, was wrestling with a much larger woman. The woman's left arm and right leg appeared to be made of metal, like robotic implants, but Daisy had interlocked her fingers with the fingers of the woman's fleshy right arm, twisting them back so fiercely Scout flinched just looking at it.

It had to hurt, given the way the much larger, half-robot woman was letting herself be guided to the exit. Then Daisy thrust her outside with such force the much larger woman fell to the ground.

"I'll be back!" she shouted, shoving a mass of flame-red hair out of her eyes to fix Daisy with a glare.

"Sleep a bit first," Daisy shouted back, then turned to look towards the youth.

And Scout.

She didn't run, but Scout doubted many could walk as fast as Daisy when she wanted to be somewhere in a hurry.

"News?" she said to Scout.

"Message," Scout said.

Daisy nodded, then turned to the youth. "Sammy—"

But he didn't even let her finish her request. "Sure, early lunch," he said with a shrug. "It's not like you haven't earned it, miss Never Takes Her Breaks."

Daisy glanced over at Scout. "It might be more than that."

"Well, I certainly hope I'll see you again, but if I don't, it's not like high turnover isn't quintessential Galactic Central," Sammy said, giving her biceps a firm grasp. "Best of luck to you."

"Thanks," Daisy said, then grasped Scout's arm and all but dragged her out of the public house.

"We have to get to the court building," Scout said. "That's all I know."

"So you didn't find Sparrow," Daisy said.

"No, got a message from Bo," Scout said.

Scout had to all but jog to keep up with Daisy as they crossed the open plaza.

The closer they got to the court building, the more it towered over them. It was the single largest building on this island and supported the largest buildings in Galactic Central.

Scout had seen smaller cities.

Daisy ran up the steps, then stopped at the massive open doorways to wait for Scout to catch up.

"Which way?" Daisy asked.

Scout, fighting to catch her breath, just shook her head. "Just said court."

Daisy frowned, looking around. Then she grabbed Scout's wrist to tow her after her into the building's lobby. One long desk of glowing wood dominated the far side of the lobby, two long staircases curving around behind it. Swarms of people were waiting in queues to speak to the clerks who stood on the far side of the desk, looking things up on tablets built into the tabletop or pointing out directions on holographic maps they handed to the visitors.

"Here," Daisy said, pulling Scout over to a computer screen built into the wall.

"Shouldn't we get in line?" Scout asked.

"That will take too long," Daisy said, then thrust her finger against a port built into the bottom of the computer screen. Her eyes flickered rapidly until, as if sensing how creepy that was for Scout, she closed them.

Daisy had memorized the maps of the city back on Schneeheim. For some reason, Scout had assumed that had involved looking at images and committing them to her photographic memory.

She kept forgetting just how much Daisy's body and brain had been augmented. Daisy was so much more than human now.

But her augments paled in comparison to what Shi Jian had coursing through her body.

"There's an office," Daisy said, turning away from the computer screen. "It's on the second level, but quite a way back."

"You can find it?" Scout asked. The computer screen was telling her nothing.

"Yes," Daisy said. "And at the top of the stairs there's a moving platform, so the five-kilometer walk won't be so bad."

"Five kilometers?" Scout repeated, but Daisy was already taking the steps two at a time. Scout followed after, acutely aware of the eyes of a security guard tracking their progress. But if there was anything unusual about two teenaged girls in the courthouse all but sprinting around the space, the guard made no move to restrain them or tell them to slow down.

The moving platform that ran down the immense hallway was more elaborate than Scout had been expecting. There were five separate belts, each moving at its own speed. Daisy stepped onto the first one, then worked her way across, stepping onto the ever faster-moving walkways until she was whizzing down the hallway. Scout progressed more slowly, terrified of what would happen if she fell. How far would she be thrown? How badly would she be damaged, flying into the stone archways that punctuated the endless hallway of dark wood doors and larger open doorways?

Daisy came back to hold out a hand and help her step onto the last, fastest platform. Scout didn't mind her holding her hand now; her heart was beating a mile a minute, and the visions of flying off the platform wouldn't leave her mind.

"One of these courtrooms is full of people deciding our fate right now," Daisy said, trying to peer into each open doorway they passed, but they never got more than a glimpse of rows of people sitting in benches, other people further forward on platforms, pontificating.

"More than our fate," Scout said. "Our whole world's. I wonder if Seeta, Geeta, and Emilie have been summoned to speak for us yet?"

"All Space Farers," Daisy said.

"That doesn't matter anymore," Scout said.

"It never did, I guess," Daisy conceded. "It was all a lie. But it was a lie that killed my parents. And yours."

"But the lie is over," Scout said. "Isn't it?"

"Only because we're facing bigger foes," Daisy said. "Here, we should start moving back across. We're nearly there."

This time she stayed close to Scout's side, not pulling her about but hovering in case Scout should need her. Scout took it one step at a time, moving to ever more slowly moving platforms until she found herself standing on immobile stone.

"This way," Daisy said, leading the way to one of the endless rows of unmarked doors of dark wood. Scout looked at it, blinked, and her glasses gave her a label: council chamber 97445, reserved for Tajaki Trade Dynasty representative Bo Tajaki and staff.

"I hope it's good news," Scout murmured. Daisy gave her a tight smile, and Scout knew she didn't think it was, but didn't want to disappoint Scout.

Then she pushed open the door, and they were inside a long, narrow room. The far wall was a series of windows overlooking some smaller interior courtyard below, a walking path between trees growing from massive urns. Across the courtyard was more of the court building, and just visible high above was the sky of pink clouds that encompassed all Galactic Central.

The table that ran down the center of the room had chairs enough for four dozen people to sit together, although how they could have anything like a council meeting with so many present Scout couldn't imagine. But at the moment, the space was empty. A few chairs at the end closest to the door were in disarray, as if a smaller number of people had just gotten up to step out for a moment. A carafe of water and a scattering of glasses were still there, condensation dripping down the sides.

"Did we just miss him?" Scout wondered, but Daisy was backing away, putting Scout's body between her and something at the far side of the table.

But when Scout looked up, the only thing there was a single man standing with his back to them as if he was looking out the window to the garden below. But instead, he had a hand pressed over his eyes.

The hand was shaking, ever so slightly.

Scout looked at the darkly tanned skin of the man's bare scalp, the white mustache just visible under the hand pressed to his eyes. The gold ring shaped like a twisted shaft of wheat.

Did she know this man?

Daisy took a step back, grabbing Scout's wrist once more to drag her out of the room, but Scout was not ready to leave yet. Bo had sent for her, and she had come, but where was he?

And why was this stranger so familiar?

Daisy tried to tug her away again, pulling hard enough to yank Scout off-balance. She grabbed the back of a chair to keep from falling over, and the legs of the chair skittered across the stone floor loudly.

Daisy made a sound that Scout would swear was a whimper if she hadn't been absolutely sure that no such sound would ever leave Daisy's throat.

The man startled at the sound, then dropped his hand and turned towards them.

Scout had been hoping for a moment of revelation, but even seeing his entire face, she still wasn't sure who he was.

His eyes on hers said he didn't know her either.

But then they moved past her to land on Daisy.

"By the stars innumerable," he said, taking half a step forward. Then, with deep anguish, "Clementine?"

And just like that, Scout knew who she was looking at. Tony Smith, father of Ruth Smith, the first person Scout had ever seen die.

The woman who had taken in Daisy's sister Clementine as her ward, a decision that had led to her murder.

Tony Smith, the governor of the world of Amatheon.

7

A SERIES of images flashed through Scout's mind: Clementine's mouth contorted in an endless scream with Ruth's too-still body beside her, the strange little device Warrior had perched on Ruth's belly to learn what had killed her.

Ruth's body wrapped in a sheet between Viola's and Liv's. Scout had stood over them, wanting to say some words but not knowing what words to say.

Scout triggering the explosives that collapsed the entire compound hidden deep under the surface of Amatheon.

But only one real thought would form in her mind, although it repeated ever faster on a desperate loop.

How much does he know?

Daisy let go of Scout's hand and straightened to her full height. Now that fleeing without being seen was no longer possible, she had no qualms about confrontation.

Scout wasn't so sure that was a good idea. She tried to keep her body between Daisy and the governor, but he brushed past her to look down at Daisy's upturned face. He raised a hand, not quite touching the strands of her closely-cut hair.

"Not Clementine," he said, but there was still a question in his eyes.

"I'm her sister, Daisy," Daisy said. "Clementine is dead."

"Yes, I know," he said. "I'm sorry for your loss."

"Your loss too," Daisy said.

"My loss, but also my fault," he said. "There are so many things I wish I could have done differently."

"Is that why you're here?" Scout asked.

He looked over at her as if suddenly noticing she was there. "You're from Amatheon as well?" he asked.

"Sunshine Valley, originally," Scout said. He flinched, recognizing the name of one of the cities destroyed in the war. "My name is Scout Shannon," she said, bracing herself, uncertain of how much he knew. But if her name was familiar to him, he didn't show it. He just nodded absentmindedly.

"You're here for the court case," Daisy persisted.

"Yes," he said. "The tribunal enforcers fetched me, right out of a council meeting. Now I'm here, but I don't think anything I say is going to make any difference. I can see it in the eyes of those three judges. They already know their answer. This is all just formality. A time-wasting formality."

"They are giving control of Amatheon to the Months," Scout said, her hands tightening into fists.

"Who?" the governor asked.

"Mai and Jun Tajaki," Scout said.

"The sisters? Oh no," he said, shaking his head with absolute surety. "No, Bo Tajaki is who we will answer to soon."

"You don't think that's the best outcome?" Scout asked.

"Absolutely," the governor said. "I've only been here for two days, but already Lord Tajaki and I have shared a great rapport. He has great ideas for improving life on Amatheon and knows exactly what my role should be in implementing them."

"So why are you so sad?" Scout asked.

"Because none of it's going to matter," he said. "The tribunal court requires my presence here for four more days. Just some formality, they say. But in four more days, life on the surface and in orbit around Amatheon will likely be destroyed."

"What do you mean?" Scout asked.

"War is breaking out, and because I'm here, there is no one there to stop it."

"War," Daisy said.

"There's a lot I didn't tell you," Scout said, her voice pitched low, but the governor looked at her intently. Clearly, he wanted her to go on. "The rebels have what your daughter was bringing to them. I tried to keep it away from them, but I couldn't. They know about the gun under construction."

"I've tried to block that monstrosity at every turn," the governor said, pressing one fist to his mouth as if to hold back his own frustrated anger. "I *did* block it, officially. Not that it mattered. Our laws no longer matter. Not even to my own council. I've long suspected they were working against me, but I didn't want to act without proof. I regret that now."

"It's going to be a three-way war," Scout said. "Planet Dwellers, Space Farers, and rebels, all fighting each other."

"No," the governor said. "Not that it matters in the bigger picture, but we lost control of that gun some time ago. And the guns that date back to the first war have fallen into disrepair. My government is out of the fight. Our people will just be collateral damage now."

"Lost control?" Daisy repeated. "How?"

"The rebels have it," Scout guessed.

The governor nodded. "It won't matter who fires it," he said. "The Space Farers will retaliate. Life on the surface will be wiped out long before I can get back there."

"So leave now," Daisy said. "I can get you a ship."

The governor's eyebrows raised. But then he shook his head. "No, it's quite impossible. I'm being monitored at all times. The tracker is irremovable. I cannot leave until the tribunal court dismisses me."

"Is there anyone back home you can get a message to? Anyone you trust?" Scout asked.

"No one, not anymore," the governor said. "Someone has been turning my council members against me, against our planet's interests. I thought it was just one or two, but I'm increasingly certain it's all of them. I don't know who or why or what they want. I just know there is no longer anyone I can trust."

"It's the Months," Scout said, looking to Daisy. "They know they're going to lose this. They would rather see it all destroyed than not own it."

"Are you sure?" the governor asked, then grasped Scout's arm to lean closer to her. "Can you prove it?"

"Yes," Scout said, but was forced to add, "and no."

The governor looked like he wanted to say more, but a clutch of Bo's lawyers came into the room. Scout saw to her surprise that they were all dressed in different colors. When she had been on Bo's ship, everyone had worn the same color to suit his whim, the color changing as his whims changed.

It seemed that he had given up a measure of control. Scout was pleased he had listened to her.

The governor released her arm and turned to the lawyers, but his release was more of a shove, a hint that she should make herself scarce. Daisy was already fading back against the wall, slipping out the door to the hallway beyond. Scout ducked her head, flittering unnoticed through the mass of chattering lawyers.

Scout was torn between relief that he didn't know she had been there when his daughter died and a more complicated, confused, disappointed sort of feeling.

Had she gotten that used to everyone just knowing who she was? Which was ridiculous. She was a bike messenger from a planet so remote it was literally sealed off from the rest of the galaxy.

Granted, he had been from the same planet, but still. And anyway, it was better that he didn't know her. It saved telling the story of every-thing that had happened in the underground compound during that solar storm.

They were back out in the hallway, and Scout looked at the moving platform, which only ran in one direction. She was just lamenting the long walk back and considering trying to bust out one of the windows so she could ride out on her glider when Daisy caught her elbow, directing her through one of the open doorways. This courtroom was empty, the only light from the hallway behind them and through another open door on the far side of the room. Beyond that door was another hallway, this one with a moving walkway running back towards the main door.

Without a word, Daisy and Scout rode the walkway until it ended, then went down the steps and back out to the plaza.

"What now?" Scout asked as Daisy led the way past the fountain. "Are you going back to work?"

"Work?" Daisy said. "No, we need to find Sparrow."

"Sparrow?"

"If your hunch is right, and it is the Months behind everything, she's our best bet to find proof."

"What good will proof do?" Scout asked. "We bring it back here, and then what? Someone is holding the governor here for no reason. We'll just end up trapped here with him. He said he can't trust anyone on Amatheon. I don't think we can trust anyone here either," Scout said.

"Maybe not," Daisy said. "But I still want reliable info before we act."

"Did you hear something about where we can find Sparrow?" Scout asked as Daisy led the way through the arches of the public house and back into the marketplace.

"No," Daisy said.

"So this is hopeless," Scout said.

"I know it's not how we wanted to play it," Daisy said. "But I'm here with you, so I think it's our best bet."

"What's our best bet?"

"We're going to let your pursuers come to us."

It took a lot longer than Scout would have liked. Soon her stomach was growling so loudly that even Daisy could hear it. She stopped at a food cart and got her a skewer of grilled fish and another of vegetables, and Scout ate as they continued to roam down the most remote, narrowest alleys they could find.

There were a lot of places in the marketplace that were ripe for an ambush. Too many.

"We should get back," Scout said some hours later. "Or at least one of us should. The dogs need to be let out."

"I guess you're right," Daisy said, disappointment clear on her face. But then the corners of her mouth quirked as if she were fighting a smile. Scout looked at her, but she just raised hands.

"We surrender," she said, and Scout turned to see five kids all dressed in black walking up behind them. She looked the other way and saw three more blocking the only other exit.

"Yes, we surrender," she said, letting one of them take her glider from her. "Take us to your leader?"

None of them said a word, just led the way down a maze of alleys to another public house. It was nowhere near as large as the one where Daisy worked, but this one too had been tunneled into the stone of the bridge itself to gain a sublevel. There were no floating platforms here, and Scout had to duck to get her head under the coarsely made wood floor as she followed the steps cut into the stone down to a dark basement.

"I hope this wasn't a bad idea," she whispered to Daisy. Daisy had enhanced hearing; Scout had to just barely speak for her to hear, only a slight rumble to her vocal cords.

But if Daisy responded in kind, Scout with her conventional ears heard nothing.

The staircase was almost completely dark, her glasses giving her the general outlines of the walls and ceiling and of the kids crowded all around her.

Then it took a turn, the steps grew wider, and she could see a warm light at the bottom.

The space had clearly been intended for storage, with dusty crates stacked all around the walls, but the center of the space had been cleared and swept clean. A single chair sat under a pair of lights, and on the chair sat a girl with an explosion of thick hair barely contained by the red hood she had pulled up to keep her face in shadow.

The minute Scout stepped into the light, she threw the hood back, launching herself off the chair to tackle Scout in a fierce hug.

"Hey, Sparrow," Scout said, patting her awkwardly on the back.

"You know, if you wanted to talk to me, you could have just told these kids to give me a message."

"It's all messed up," Sparrow said. She wasn't crying, but she was very close to it. "It's all so, so messed up."

"The Months?" Daisy asked, and Sparrow looked over at her.

"This is Daisy," Scout said. "A friend. Daisy, this is Sparrow."

Sparrow looked her over. By the time she was done assessing her, she had her emotions back under control. She returned to her chair under the lights but left her hood thrown back.

"Yes," she said. "The Months."

"You know about the war that's about to break out," Scout pressed.

"Probably more details than you do," Sparrow said.

"You still work for the Months?" Scout asked.

"I bring food to your friends twice a day," Sparrow said. "The rest of the time, no one cares where I am. So I've been snooping."

"Were they called to testify?" Scout asked.

"Yes, but they didn't go to the court building to do it. It was done remotely. It could have been done from home," Sparrow said bitterly.

"Daisy and I have a way to get them out," Scout said.

"And we have a ship that will take us back to Amatheon," Daisy said, which was news to Scout.

"Those are good things," Sparrow said. "But they aren't going to matter a bit if you don't have a way past the blockade, which is still standing. Or a way to get on board *Amatheon Orbiter 1* or down to the surface without being detected by the Space Farers or the rebels."

"It'll probably be easier just to get caught," Scout said. "It worked to get us to you."

"It won't work for this," Sparrow said. "I'm not your enemy. They are."

"You already have a plan," Daisy said, and Sparrow narrowed her eyes at her for a long minute before breaking out in a broad smile.

"I do indeed have a plan," she said. "More than that, I have allies."

"Who?" Scout asked. The last she had seen, Sparrow had been a tiny presence lost among the pirates that flocked around the Months. She had passed her time befriending the crew in engineering. How could engineers help now?

Sparrow pulled a cloth with a flourish to reveal a communications screen, and Scout realized even as her eyes confirmed it just who Sparrow had been plotting with.

Tom Tom. The pilot Sparrow had introduced her to in an arcade back on the Months' ship.

The pilot that had run missions between the Months in orbit and the rebels down on the surface.

8

"SPARROW? YOU'RE BACK?" Tom Tom asked, flicking the long, dark blond bangs back from his eyes. Sparrow stepped directly in front of the screen, and his eyes focused on her. "There you are."

"And I'm not alone," Sparrow told him, extending a hand back behind her. Scout looked at it but didn't take it.

Allies. Plural. Not just Tom Tom.

Daisy was looking at her, one eyebrow raised in an unasked question. But it wasn't like Scout could explain right now, surrounded by strangers and within Tom Tom's hearing.

Scout sighed and put her hand in Sparrow's, letting the younger girl drag her forward.

Tom Tom visibly perked up. "Scout Shannon!" he said. "You fell off everybody's radar for a while there. Some thought you were dead."

"I wasn't," Scout said.

"I never believed it," Sparrow said with fierce loyalty.

"Who did?" Scout wondered.

Sparrow frowned in thought. "Mai. Or at least she really hoped it was true," she said. "Jun insisted it couldn't be, though. Out of the two of them, I tend to trust Jun."

Scout was surprised by that. The two sisters looked alike, although they weren't quite twins, but their temperaments could not have been more opposite. Mai did all the talking, strove to appear reasonable, always wanted to make a deal that would at least seem to be in everyone's best interests.

But Jun was a creature of raw emotion. She seldom spoke, but she did enjoy throwing things.

The more she thought about it, the more Scout would have to agree with Sparrow that Jun was the more trustworthy of the two. She had no layers, no place where she hid things. She thought it, she acted on it, in the most explosive manner possible.

But whatever intel they had gotten about all that had happened on Schneeheim must have been vague indeed for the two sisters to come to such opposite conclusions. Scout supposed that was good for her.

"I've been trying to bring Scout and her friend…"

"Daisy," Scout said.

"Her friend Daisy up to speed with our plans," Sparrow said to Tom Tom, who nodded, still preferring just to listen. "The Months are heading back to Amatheon sometime tonight. The easiest, most direct way for us to get there is for me to maintain my guise as a member of their crew, and for you two to sneak on board. I can get you in with the food shipment, no problem. The kitchen crew likes me; the Months, not so much."

"The Months' ship," Scout repeated, her tone carefully neutral. She had been on the Months' ship before when it was waiting to cross the barricade to leave Amatheon. It was like a floating city, complete with a hospital, a walking park under an artificial sun, a marketplace, and a pirate court that flocked around the Months, looking to curry favor.

On board the Months' ship, she had had her first encounter with a warp engine. It had had strange effects on her, as if it had tried to pull her into a dream. But she had not traveled at warp speeds on that ship.

Would warp on their ship be like when she traveled with the tribunal enforcers? That warp field had made her feel oddly out of sorts, but the mild sensation of wrongness had died the moment they had left warp. That would be livable to experience again.

But what if it was like the ship they stole from Shi Jian, with its ultrafast warp technology? In that warp field, Scout had felt beyond disoriented, scarcely able to walk. Her brain insisted she was constantly tumbling forward at high speeds. And more than a few minutes of that had made even maintaining consciousness a challenge.

And it had taken weeks to recover from the experience. What would be the point of reaching Amatheon if she was useless until after everything was all over, for good or ill?

And what if it didn't matter what kind of engine it was this time? What if her last experience in a warp field had changed something in her brain, had made any warp travel debilitating for her now?

She wouldn't know for sure until she tried it. It was going to be a huge risk.

"Scout?" Sparrow asked.

But the frown on Daisy's face didn't have the same confusion in it. "What about the dogs?" she asked.

"The dogs," Sparrow repeated as if she had just remembered that they existed.

"The dogs," Scout said, trying not to sound like she had forgotten them herself. But they were a consideration too. "Smuggling them in through a kitchen is going to be much harder. We'll be much likelier to be caught."

"Can't you leave them behind?" Tom Tom asked, and Scout shot him a glare. "Not forever, just until you get back," he quickly amended.

Scout didn't answer. In her life, getting back to places was never a given. There was no way she would leave her dogs behind.

"I already have a ship lined up for us to travel in," Daisy said. "I hired the whole ship out, so we won't have to hide, and the dogs will be with us openly."

"So, you two go out on that and meet us at Amatheon," Sparrow said, tapping a fingernail against her teeth as she pondered.

"It's already getting too complicated," Tom Tom said. "Multiple pickups?"

"You were already planning multiple drop-offs," Scout pointed out.

"We should stick together," Daisy said. "Scout and I have been working on a plan to bust your three friends out of the Months' compound since we got here. We've worked out every detail, practiced every skill that will be required. To wait to break them out of a ship that's unfamiliar to me... I don't like those odds."

"I agree," Scout said. "We should get them now."

"That might work," Sparrow said, her voice muffled as she continued to tap her teeth. "Yes, I can swing it. I'm in charge of the three of them, sort of. If you get them out tonight, I can help. I'll make the compound people think they've already gone up to the ship. I might even be able to trick the ship's systems into thinking they're already up there. That won't last, but it might last until they've gone to warp. They are in a hurry."

"You can do it?" Scout asked. Sparrow still looked unsure.

Sparrow furrowed her brow, but then she dropped her hand away from her mouth and broke out in a wide grin. "Yes, I can."

"Then we'll arrange for our ship and get the dogs on board. After that, we'll get the three of them out," Daisy said.

"You'll be with them? You'll come with us?" Scout asked.

"Of course," Sparrow said. "Then Tom Tom will meet your ship, and we can work out from there who's going where."

"It makes the most sense for your three Space Farer friends to head to *Amatheon Orbiter 1*, while Scout and I go down to the surface," Daisy said.

"And you should go with them," Scout said to Sparrow, as Daisy apparently didn't realize the girl was also a Space Farer.

"The groups aren't equal," Sparrow frowned.

"Won't matter," Tom Tom said from up on the screen. "We're meeting with allies in both places. They need your intel, not your physical bodies."

"You have secret ways to get us where we're going?" Scout asked.

"For the space station, we'll go in through the impound lot."

Scout bit her lip but nodded, ignoring Daisy's look of concern. Shi Jian had thrown Seeta out through that airlock when Scout and her friends were attempting to flee that station. Seeta had all but died. Just the idea of going back there gave Scout the shivers.

But she wouldn't be going back there. She was on the other team.

"And on the planet?" she asked.

"The rebels have moved since you were with them," Tom Tom said.

"They're higher in the mountains now, closer to the gun. But there's a hidden hangar deck on the opposite side of the mountain peak from their encampment. It will take some fancy flying on my part, but that's no problem."

Scout was still lost in thought and didn't really register the glow of self-pride he was radiating. Not until Daisy noticed it and gave him a scowl. Tom Tom slumped a bit.

"We'll land on the hangar deck. Then what?" Scout asked.

"I'll be off again, but you'll be in good hands," he said.

"Good hands," Scout repeated. "Whose hands?"

"The best of hands," Tom Tom said hurriedly. "He can get you inside with no one the wiser and take you directly to anywhere you need to go. He's willing to do anything you need and will give his life if that's what it takes to keep you safe."

Scout felt Daisy's eyes on her, questioning, but she felt too many other eyes also on her and kept her expression guarded. Daisy turned back to Tom Tom.

"I know we just met, and I don't really know any of you, but it sounds like you're being deliberately vague. I have to wonder, with all that's going on, why?" Daisy said.

"Because it's Tucker," Scout said with a sigh, "isn't it?"

"Yes," Tom Tom said. He looked like he was ready to flinch if she struck out at him, which was ridiculous given how many light-years there were between them.

"Is this a problem?" Sparrow asked.

"What about someone else?" Scout asked. "Joelle is better connected and far more capable. I would even trust Ken or Bente more," Scout said.

"Look, it has to be Tucker," Tom Tom said. "And you know how sorry he is for everything that happened. He's risking a lot helping you out with this. He's doing it because he feels like he owes it to you."

"He doesn't owe me anything," Scout said.

"Not *you* you," Tom Tom said hastily, although Scout knew that was exactly what he had meant. "The… all of you, doing what you're doing now to stop the war. I guess we can't call you rebels, since there already are rebels. Disruptors, maybe?"

"We don't need a name," Daisy said.

"He owes it to you. Anything he can do up to sacrificing his own life. To stop the war," Tom Tom said. Scout was certain he could continue spouting out short, choppy sentences forever until she gave in.

"Scout? Is this going to be a problem?" Sparrow asked. Her eyes were wide with worry. She had spent a lot of time working on the plan for this. She had invested a lot of emotion in it too. Scout remembered she had just lost her brother. Had she pushed her grief aside to focus on this?

Daisy was looking at her too, her eyebrows raised as she waited for Scout to answer. Scout could see the same feeling in her eyes that she felt herself. What she wouldn't give for a quiet, spy-free space and five minutes alone with her best friend to talk it all over before she decided.

But she was never going to get that.

"No," Scout gave in with a sigh. "It's not going to be a problem." She'd find a way to deal with it. Starting with never being alone with the boy who had betrayed her. She didn't care what he was willing to do; nothing was going to take back what he had done.

"Then it's all settled?" Sparrow asked. She still sounded anxious.

"It better be," Daisy said. "We don't have much time. Scout and I will get the dogs on the ship, then break into the compound. You do what you need to do on your end, and we'll see you there…"

"At 2000 hours," Sparrow said. "Just long enough past the dinner hour for things to be settling down in the compound, but not so soon that anyone will be checking for what's been left behind before the ship departs."

"Then we'll see you then," Daisy said. She gave a tight smile to Sparrow, then an unsmiling glance up at Tom Tom still on the communications screen.

Scout let herself be guided back up to street level. She half expected it to be dark when they emerged, but even if it had been the middle of the night, the sky would still have the same rosy glow. That never changed.

"I hope you weren't bluffing about having a ship," Scout said.

"Of course not," Daisy said, not quite sounding offended. "I set up that contract days ago with some of the money from selling the other ship. I picked that public house to work in for a reason."

"All the ship crews drink there," Scout guessed.

"Not just crew, captains," Daisy said. "And I have one who's agreed to leave at a moment's notice, to take us and the dogs and however many passengers we require to Amatheon. Her name is Jocquette Dieu-le-Veut."

"And we can trust this Captain Dieu-le-Veut?" Scout asked. She thought of the people she had seen that morning hunched over tables. Had anyone there struck her eye as being noble or trustworthy?

"You actually sort of met her already," Daisy said.

Scout gave her a puzzled glance. She couldn't mean Sammy. Aside from being clearly an employee of that public house, Sammy had been a he.

Slowly, it dawned on her who Daisy was eluding to.

Away from the gazes of strangers, Scout made no effort to keep her feelings from washing over her face.

"Scout, it's going to be fine," Daisy assured her. "She was a bit drunk this morning, sure, but she'll be fine now. When you saw me throw her out of the house, I was reminding her she was being paid to be ready at all times. I'm sure she took that to heart."

Scout said nothing. Somehow, it wasn't the worst revelation of the last several minutes.

After all, this drunk captain hadn't actually betrayed her. Yet.

9

THE DOGS WERE ecstatic to see both of them coming home at once. Scout took them down to the cave to run off all the energy they could, and by the time she took them back to the room, Daisy had what few belongings that mattered to them packed in a small, sealed plastic crate.

There was another crate beside it, a bit larger, with small holes drilled through it in several places. Daisy dropped to her knees, and Gert ran to her, tail wagging so hard the motion started at her forelegs. Daisy snuggled her and petted her and cooed over her, then snatched her up and stuffed her inside the crate. Scout scooped up Shadow and pushed Gert to one side to make room for him. Before either of them knew quite what was going on, Daisy had shut the lid and sealed it shut.

"How do we do this?" Scout asked, looking from the delicate glider in her hand to the two crates they had to carry.

"I'll show you," Daisy said. "You'll get the hang of it once we're out in free fall. I'll take the dogs. If you have to ditch your crate, we'll get by, but I'm sure you'll be fine."

Scout nodded, far less sure herself.

Daisy hefted the crate with both dogs inside and carried it out the doorway, down the hall to the tunnel on the far side of the cave. Scout, carrying the smaller, far lighter crate, envied how easy Daisy made it look. Sure, her augmented body had super strength, but how did she manage to slip through the narrowest parts of the end of the cave as if the plastic crate in her arms was as fluid as her own body?

Daisy came back and helped Scout angle her own crate through the narrowest bit. If she too was wondering how Scout was going to manage flying with a box she couldn't walk with, she didn't show it.

Once they were out on the sandy patch outside of the tunnel mouth, Daisy stopped to pull a rope harness out of one of her cargo pockets. Scout had one just like it in one of her belt pouches, and she quickly slipped it over her shoulders and fastened it in front. Scout waited for Daisy to attach hers to the crate, but instead, she turned to Scout.

"You first," Daisy said.

"Me first? I don't know what I'm doing."

"You first so I can help you," Daisy said, adjusting the fit of Scout's harness before running a rope through the ring set over her breast-bone. "I'm giving you a lot of extra length. You have a sense of how far down the artificial gravity goes here?"

"Sort of," Scout said.

"You'll jump out and get your wind under you; then I'll toss down the crate. It's going to drag you down. Don't worry about that. Just keep yourself level. Once you're out of the gravity field, everything is going to feel much more natural."

Scout doubted that. She would still have a lot of extra mass dangling at the end of a long rope. Non-aerodynamic mass at that.

Scout waited for Daisy to give her a nod, then took as much of a run as she could, launching off the last bit of rock and extending her glider wings to catch the air.

It felt like her best takeoff ever, right up until Daisy tossed down the crate.

Scout could tell that Daisy had thrust it as straight down as she could with all of her augmented strength, sending it on the fastest path out of the gravity field rather than swinging it on the end of its rope, a motion that would likely send Scout tumbling out of proper glider configuration. Even so, the sudden increase in weight made her all too aware that her body weight was being held aloft by what basically amounted to plastic paper.

But she remembered what Daisy said and fought the urge to panic at how fast the underbelly of island bedrock was zooming past her, focusing instead on keeping her arms spread wide, letting her wings fill with air. She caught an updraft just as she plunged out of the gravity field, not enough to buoy her back up again but enough to let her circle in place for a moment, to get used to the odd pendulum of mass confusing her momentum.

Then Daisy was beside her. The dogs in their crate were fastened flush against her belly. Not that they found that comforting: even with the wind filling her ears, Scout could hear their anxious whining.

"Got it?" Daisy asked, drawing close to Scout's side.

"I think so," Scout said. "Is it far to this port?"

Daisy laughed. "We're in the middle of a spherical cloud, and all the ports are on the edge."

Scout laughed in return. Galactic Central had many spaceports, the largest positioned "above" the two main islands at the "top" of the cloud. Given that "up" and "down" were largely defined by everyone on the islands choosing to orient their islands with their unique gravity fields the same way, the distinction was purely academic. And given that no edge of the bubble that contained the atmosphere was any closer to the central islands than any other edge, the main port being on the edge directly overhead was doubly academic.

But there were many other ports all around the edges of the bubble, most grouped together by common interests. Trading ships mostly moved in and out of one cluster of ports, passenger vessels another.

Scout didn't know which port they had come in through, only that Daisy had been able to dock a stolen ship there, get Scout and the dogs off, and exchange that ship for a stack of coins before the authorities were any the wiser. Scout expected where they were going would prove to be, if not the same place, a very similar one.

And indeed, Daisy led her to a small, isolated port, as far from the part of the cloud the Tajaki trade dynasty inhabited as it was possible to get, and not part of any cluster. The island they landed on was barely more than a bare patch of rock, just large enough to hold the half of the building that stood within the contained atmosphere. There was just room enough for them to touch down and fold their gliders before entering the doorway to the dark interior.

The place looked like it had seen better days. The waiting area was ample, but there was nowhere to sit. Scout could see marks on the floor showing where benches had once been bolted down. Now there was nothing but skittering dust bunnies that danced across the floor to pile up closer to the walls.

The storage rooms, on the other hand, were packed to maximum capacity. And someone was lingering in each of those doorways, not waiting, just watching as Daisy and Scout continued down the long hall.

The vaulted roof had an occasional skylight, the only sources of light in the space. One pair of skylights, Scout was still looking up into the pinkish gray cloud that encased Galactic Central. The next she was looking up into the black of space.

"This way," Daisy said, as the main hallway split off into a web of smaller corridors. They climbed a ramp and went down another long corridor that ended in an open airlock.

"Captain Dieu-le-Veut!" Daisy called, catching Scout by the arm to keep her from stepping through the airlock.

"Who wants to know?" a woman called back. It didn't sound like her mood had improved since Scout had seen her last, on the ground outside the public house.

"Ruby Peach," Daisy called back, then made a little face at Scout, as if flinching at her own alias.

"Ruby Peach owes me money," the captain snarled.

"Not yet, she doesn't," Daisy said. "Permission to come aboard?"

"Cheeky!" the captain snapped. Then Scout heard a metallic clang and imagined a hand grasping a ship's bulkhead to pull a body up out of a chair, then a deeper series of clangs as her steps drew ever nearer.

It looked like they had woken her up. Her flame-red hair had pulled loose from its braid, dancing in a cloud around her head as she ducked inside her ship's airlock to glare out at them.

"Who's this?" she demanded.

"Passenger," Daisy said. "You're about to get the second installment as soon as we get these crates on board. But you're not to leave and spend it on wine. We'll be leaving in a hurry once we have the other passengers with us."

"This job is starting to sound like more trouble than it's worth," the captain grumbled.

"It's exactly what we agreed to," Daisy said reasonably.

"Maybe I give back the advance and we call it even," the captain said. "It's not like I'll have an opportunity for cargo or work out the way you're going."

"Fine," Daisy said brightly, ignoring Scout's jaw dropping open. It was far too late to start changing the plan now. But she remained silent. Surely Daisy knew what she was doing. "If you just fetch the money, I'll count to see that it's all there, and we'll be on our way."

"Well," the captain said. "We did have an arrangement, as you said. You can stack your crates through there, in storage, and pay me the second bit as promised."

"You can't leave the ship while we're gone," Daisy said firmly.

"I do believe I only agreed not to leave the port," the captain said testily.

Scout cast her mind back to her short walk through the port. She hadn't seen any sort of dining or drinking establishment, but surely there must have been something tucked away in a corner...?

"You have to stay in the ship," Daisy said, pulling Scout in after her so she could shut the airlock door. "We have something that requires looking after."

"That wasn't part of the agreement," the captain all but snarled.

Daisy didn't respond, just bent to open the larger of the two crates, the one containing Shadow and Gert. They came bounding out to run to Scout, then skidded to a halt when they saw the stranger towering over them.

All the anger drained out of her face. For a minute, Scout thought she saw sadness there. But then a smile appeared as she dropped down to one knee and held out her hands. Not a particularly friendly smile, not one that seemed to get much use, but the dogs only recognized that someone wanted to be friends. They approached cautiously, both eschewing the metallic hand in favor of the fleshy one. The captain spoke comforting words to them in a language Scout didn't recognize.

"We won't be long," Daisy said. "All of our stuff is in the other crate, and our friends will be traveling light."

The captain didn't seem to hear, lost as she was in scratching first one dog's ears, then the other's.

"We'll be in a significant hurry when we return," Daisy persisted.

"I'll be ready," the captain said. It sounded like she wanted it to come out more snappish than it did, but she couldn't manage that and smile at the dogs at the same time. "Don't worry about us. We'll be fine."

Daisy and Scout slipped out of the airlock, closing the door behind them before the dogs could quite figure out what was going on.

"You're sure we can trust her?" Scout asked. She hated leaving her dogs with strangers.

"Captain Jocquette Dieu-le-Veut has no friends or family and seldom works with a crew," Daisy told her as she wrapped her arm around Scout's and led her back out of the port. "What she did have was a dog. Decades old, that dog was, and her only companion. She's been out of sorts since he died. When I first saw her in the public house, she was mourning his death. That's how we got to talking. I would trust her with any dog's life implicitly."

"What about our lives?" Scout asked.

"We can trust her greed," Daisy said. "As long as we have money she wants that she doesn't get until the end, she'll do the job."

Scout didn't say anything. It truly was far too late to start changing the plan.

But if Captain Jocquette Dieu-le-Veut were truly motivated by money above all things, why hadn't she noticed that Daisy hadn't paid the second installment before they had left?

10

AS MUCH AS Daisy insisted that with the technology the Months had access to, it made no difference, Scout still longed for the cover of darkness. If only they could wait for nightfall to sneak inside, she wouldn't feel so exposed.

But there was no nightfall here. Only the constant pink gloaming that never quite felt like day either.

Daisy had made enough close passes to the compound to know the Months' security team tracked all glider traffic around their island and had no compunctions against stunning teenagers who drifted too close.

But the workaround she had come up with still terrified Scout.

"You're sure these will work?" Scout asked as they traced lazy circles around each other. They were so far below the bottom of the Months' island that it was a barely visible black dot above them. Then a frond of gray cloud drifted between the two of them and their target, and she couldn't see it at all.

"I wish we could have practiced more," Daisy said. "But that might have tipped our hands. Just remember, we worked out every bit of the plan. You'll be fine. And if not, I brought a spare glider for each of us, along with the ones for the others."

She tapped the bottom end of the canister strapped across her back beneath her own glider.

Scout wasn't reassured.

"I can go first," Daisy offered.

"Talk me through it one more time," Scout said, examining the frankly frightening equipment she had let Daisy strap around her waist. She had thought dangling a crate on a line had been hairy enough.

"Dive down to get speed," Daisy said, counting off steps on her fingers even as she banked around Scout. She flew with such ease she made her winged glider seem like a mere fashion accessory. "Pull up sharp, tuck your wings in tight, and then before you lose momentum, fire the rocket."

Scout gulped hard.

"We've studied the layout together a million times. I know you can find the drainage gate we're aiming for," Daisy said.

Scout managed a small nod. She had indeed studied the schematics and images from Daisy's own optical implants, but that wasn't the same as actually seeing it. Daisy had seen it, just once, just before the security team had stunned her and left her to fall.

Her version of events after that moment had been a bit muddled. But she had somehow made it back alive, so...

"We're not trying to get through it under rocket power," Daisy said. "It's just one big push at the bottom, and you let the momentum take you up. At the bottom of the island, the effects of the gravity field will negate that moment. Just catch hold of the grate before it does."

Scout gave an even tinier nod.

Daisy wasn't the only one who wished they had had time to practice. Scout didn't even know how to make her body do those things.

"Okay, I'm off," Daisy said. She spread her wings wide, feeling for the swelling of air beneath her to drop away. Then she gave Scout a wink and dove.

It looked like she had already tucked her wings away, her silhouette like an arrow as she plunged through scatters of cloud and fog. But then she spread them wide again, the arc at the bottom of her motion so tight it was almost like she was a ball bouncing back up to some kid's hand.

Then there was a flare of light, too bright to look directly at. Scout's glasses compensated just in time for her to see Daisy shoot up past her, almost within reach, but moving impossibly fast.

Scout could hear her shrieking in delight, the sound dopplering up and away from her.

Then it was her turn. Finding the swell of air and diving down the far side she had done many times before. Even banking back up again as sharply as she could was a practiced move. It was all part of what Daisy had taught her that first flying lesson, in case she should ever need to evade capture.

Then she aligned herself vertically once more, the bottom of the Months' compound somewhere in front of her, although it was once more lost in the clouds. Scout took a deep breath, shut her wings with a snap, then triggered the rocket.

Her screams were much less joyful. The intense speed, the way the force of it shook her entire body so that even the bones in her ears were jangling together—that she had expected. But the warmth spreading across her backside?

Were her pants on fire?

Thick clouds wrapped around her, cooling her entire body, and the sensation disappeared. The rocket was now just dead weight strapped around her waist. The wet droplets that struck her upturned face were like little needles, collecting on her glasses faster than the lenses could compensate.

Then she was out of the cloud and could see the bottom of the island zooming down to meet her. She was far closer than she thought she was. She quickly focused on the formations of the bedrock, jagged as if it had been ripped from a planet like a child's tooth.

A flash of color caught her attention: Daisy waving a red scarf her way. Scout realized she was a couple of meters off target but had no idea how she was supposed to steer. If she deployed her wings at this speed, they would just rip to tatters.

She reached out her hands in front of her. But she knew that wasn't going to do any good if she crashed into rock at this speed.

Then she was inside the island's gravity field. She had expected a gradual slowing of her momentum. What she got instead was a lurching halt, quickly followed by the sensation of falling.

She could taste a bitter metallic taste in the back of her mouth, as if the panic inside her were trying to well up out of her. But she swallowed hard, reached for her belt, and fired her last cable. The anchor buried itself deeply into the rock about a meter off from Daisy's position.

Scout didn't risk a look around, just focused on getting up the cable to the safety of the bedrock. She knew the whole point of the rockets had been to move too fast for the security systems to recognize them as a threat.

She definitely wasn't moving too fast now.

But she was moving faster, and when she did dare to look up from her hands pulling and grasping, pulling and grasping, she saw Daisy had opened the grate and was standing over it, reeling up the other end of the cable even as Scout continued climbing it.

She caught Scout's hand and guided it to the edge of the grate. Then she grabbed Scout under the armpits to help haul her up, then the back of her pants to all but toss her across the darkness beyond the grate.

Then the grate slammed down with a clang, and Daisy let her breath out in a whoosh.

"Guards?" Scout whispered.

"They didn't see you," Daisy said, her voice pitched even lower than Scout's. She was looking through the grate, and the light from the sky beyond lit up her face, then fluttered as three shadows crossed. But they didn't stop.

"We're good," Daisy said as Scout got to her feet and detached the cable from her belt. Her glasses adjusted to the darkness. They were in a small, squared-off space, something between a cave and a room. Crates and sacks were stacked against the walls but were covered in such thick blankets of dust they must have been forgotten centuries before.

"This way," Daisy said, and Scout followed her down a narrow hallway. She could hear the sound of running water long before the hallway ended in a catwalk with no railings that extended over an open channel of water.

"What is this?" Scout asked.

"Probably for the ponds and fountains, since it doesn't look like it's being processed," Daisy said. She walked across the narrow bridge as if she didn't even notice that nothing was keeping her body from falling over the side down into the churning water below. There was a panel in the wall on the far side, and she headed immediately for that, popping it open and tinkering at the insides and never once looking back to see if Scout followed.

Scout looked down at the water. It couldn't be so very deep, considering Scout had just come up through the very bottom of this island and hadn't gone up so much as a flight of stairs since.

Still, water moving that fast? Probably didn't need to be deep.

Back home on Amatheon, she had traveled across endless prairies, over hills and mountains and all kinds of terrain.

But she had never tried to cross a river. She had sat on the banks of one once, watching debris from a storm washing past her, getting pulled under the waves and dashed against the rocks. She had decided that her world was big enough on the side of the river she'd been born on.

But her friends were waiting for her. Daisy would be waiting for her as soon as she noticed she wasn't right behind her.

Scout took a deep breath, tuned out the angry sounds the water was making, and fixed her gaze at a point on the wall directly across from her.

She took one step after another, fighting the urge to clench her hands into fists and the even greater urge to just shut her eyes.

Then she was across. A small victory, but she would take it.

Daisy slammed the panel door shut angrily, then turned to look at Scout. Her eyebrows rose questioningly, and Scout realized she was grinning. She sterned up her facial expression.

"Problem?"

"Maybe," Daisy said. "I'm not seeing what I want to see. It might not be a problem. But then again, it might."

"Okay, what's the next step?" Scout asked.

"You wait here," Daisy said. "I'm going to go ahead a bit and make sure we're as invisible to the security systems as we're supposed to be. I'll come back for you when I'm sure."

"Okay," Scout said. She understood why Daisy would go first and alone. Being both augmented and a trained assassin, she had ways of not being seen that Scout could never learn. But... "What if you don't come back?"

"I don't know, Scout," Daisy admitted. "Let's assume I will."

"Okay," Scout said, trying to sound far surer than she felt. "I trust you."

"I trust *you*," Daisy said, squeezing her shoulder and touching her forehead to Scout's.

Then she was gone, and Scout was alone in the dark next to the chasm of raging water.

Scout tried pacing, but even this far from the edge, visions of tripping and falling into that channel tormented her. She opted instead to sit just inside the mouth of the tunnel Daisy had disappeared down.

She patted all her pockets until she found a packet of dried berries she had bought in the marketplace days before. She ate them slowly, trying to guess in the darkness which kind of berry each was without getting her glasses out to tell her.

Then the berries were all gone, and she had nothing left to do but wait.

Wait and worry.

"Hello, Teacher," she said at last.

"Hello, Scout," Warrior said, appearing at her side. Scout almost thought she could feel the warmth of her hip so close to her own, but of course, that was impossible. She was just a trick of the light, only visible to Scout because she had special glasses over her quite ordinary eyes.

"Is this going to work?" Scout asked, trying not to sound as miserable as she felt.

"Certainly," Warrior said brightly.

"How can you know that for sure?" Scout asked. The AI wasn't programmed to lie to her to make her feel better, which only made her answer more puzzling to Scout.

"I have access to the Months' systems," Warrior said. "Daisy's ploy was successful, as I'm sure she knows by now. Really, things for both of you would go so much smoother if you just told her about me."

"I can't," Scout said. "At this point, it would just be weird."

"It will only get weirder until it becomes an actual problem," Warrior said.

"I know," Scout said. "It's just—"

But Warrior winked out of existence even as Scout was looking at her. Then she saw Daisy jogging up the tunnel.

"Were you talking to someone?" Daisy asked in a whisper.

"Just myself," Scout said. "You were gone a long time."

"I ran into Sparrow," Daisy said, pressing a bundle of cloth into Scout's hands. "She gave me these. We'll just put them on over our clothes. Everything is so hectic up there, I don't think anyone would notice."

"What is it?" Scout asked, shaking it out. It appeared to be a long, white robe with sleeves so large they actually contained little pockets.

"The servants wear them," Daisy said. "I can't tell if we're invisible to the systems or not, and I asked Sparrow to find out for sure, but then she came up with this idea, which is really much simpler."

"Much," Scout agreed. She hoped Daisy's augmented eyes couldn't tell she was blushing with shame in the darkness. She told herself it didn't really matter that she wasn't telling Daisy she knew their ploy had worked, not now that they had this other, better plan.

"Follow me," Daisy said. "Sparrow is waiting at the end of this hall."

Scout wanted to argue that a slash in the bedrock hardly qualified as a hall, but the further they walked, the more squared off the walls became. Then there was light ahead of them, and then they were out in a proper hall, a large hall that looked like it had been carved out of an enormous block of rose-colored marble, complete with arches over the doorways and little statuary growing up out of the floor.

Sparrow was waiting for them, wearing a long white robe the same as theirs. She handed Daisy a tall stack of bed linens, then picked up a tray covered with plates under shiny domes from a little table and pressed it into Scout's hands.

Then she brushed past Scout to swing shut a heavy door that, once closed, proved to be shaped like a marble pillar, blending imperceptibly with the wall.

"We should hurry," Sparrow said, and there was a tightness around her eyes and mouth that spoke of great worry. Scout clutched the tray tightly to keep the domes from rattling on the plates as Sparrow, an enormous urn hugged tight to her chest, all but ran through a maze of hallways to one of the more ornate doorways.

Two guards flanked the doorway. Or Scout assumed they were guards; they had no uniforms. The motley array of bright clothing and too-generous glimpses of bare chest brought to mind the time she had been summoned before the Months and their full court of smugglers and pirates.

Sparrow gave the guards an imperious stare but said not a word. The younger of the two flushed, mumbled an apology, and opened the door for her. Sparrow straightened her back and tossed her head, but even then, the top of her tall Afro barely came to the boy's shoulder.

But her attitude made her seem taller.

Daisy and Scout rushed to follow her. Daisy glanced around, saw a row of beds against a wall, and crossed the room to set the linens there. Scout followed Sparrow to a large, round table, setting her immense tray next to the large urn.

Then she looked up and saw Emilie standing in the open archway between the room and the garden beyond. Geeta and Seeta were just behind her, Seeta holding Geeta's arm without quite leaning on her.

Scout wanted to rush forward, to throw her arms around all three of them, but Emilie's eyes were narrowed, and her head gave the smallest of shakes.

"Honestly," Sparrow said, spinning on her heel to march back to the guards at the door. "I know this isn't your usual duty, but do try a bit harder."

"How's that?" the younger asked.

"Shut the door, heathen," Sparrow all but seethed.

"Oh. Sorry," he said. His companion just rolled his eyes, although whether at him or Sparrow, it was hard to tell.

The door slowly swung closed, the guard grunting with the effort made no easier by the loudly protesting hinges.

Then it shut with a boom, as if they were all now sealed inside an airless tomb for all time.

But that macabre image didn't live long in Scout's mind. Not with all her friends around her, hugging her tightly.

"It's great to see you, don't get me wrong," Emilie said after a far briefer hug than the other two had given her. "But we have a problem."

"Yes," Scout said. "War."

"Not just that," Sparrow said sadly.

"The woman in black," Emilie said.

"Shi Jian," Scout said to Daisy. "She means Shi Jian."

11

SCOUT HAD NEVER SEEN Emilie look so thoroughly exhausted and wired with energy at the same time. Some degree of those things was sort of her trademark, but never anything like the way she looked now. Too thin, too pale, too twitchy. Her shock of red hair had faded to a yellowish pink, white at the ends and dark brown at the roots. Scout hadn't realized how carefully crafted her riot of curls had been until she saw it now in its matted, unkempt state.

She was watching Scout closely for her reaction to that name, the eyes behind those familiar dark frames wide, the pupils jumping back and forth.

"We have to get out of here," Scout said at last. It made her heart hurt just looking at her friend. Watching from above, she hadn't had a clue how bad things had gotten. She hadn't even noticed the hair.

She had been so oblivious.

"Not just yet," Sparrow said. "We're supposed to leave with empty trays. The guards will check."

"I'm not hungry," Emilie said, turning away before Sparrow had even taken the domes off the dishes. The food smelled wonderful, rich roasted meats and vegetables swimming in buttery sauce with plenty of crusty bread.

But Scout found she wasn't hungry either. Not that a handful of dried berries was enough to top her off, just that the idea of eating such heavy food when she was geared up to flee just felt wrong.

"We have to eat it," Seeta said, pulling a chair up to the table and filling a plate with a bit from each dish.

"You look good," Scout said.

"My sister takes good care of me," Seeta said with a smile. She was the very opposite of Emilie, well fed with a healthy glow. There was a slight tremor to her hand when she lifted a spoonful of sprouts onto her own plate. Geeta saw Scout frown at it and gave her a small smile and a tilt to her head that seemed to say, "Much better, but not 100 percent yet."

"We should all try to eat something," Daisy said. "We'll need the fuel for when we run."

"It's safe to come over here, you know," Sparrow said.

"Surveillance?" Daisy asked.

"All over," Sparrow said, perhaps too cheerily. "But you spoofed the system, right?"

"I'm not sure," Daisy said.

"I am," Scout said, and felt her cheeks flush again. But she held out a hand for Daisy to join them at the table. "Daisy, this is Geeta and Seeta Malini, and Emilie Tonnelier," Scout said. "Which you already know since we've been watching you all for weeks now, but now we're finally all face to face."

"Hi," Daisy said and ducked her head shyly.

"And this is Daisy," Scout said. "She saved my life, and I guess I saved hers too, but she's saved mine more."

"Pleased to meet you, Daisy," Geeta said, extending a hand. Seeta wiped her own on a napkin before holding it out as well. Emilie seemed occupied with something in the corner of the room and didn't turn around.

"You're from… what planet were you on?" Geeta asked, her gaze moving from Daisy to Scout.

"I was on a place called Schneeheim, but Daisy is actually also from Amatheon. A Planet Dweller, like me," Scout said.

"Really?" Geeta said with keen interest.

"That's not all she is," Emilie mumbled over her shoulder.

"No, that's not," Daisy agreed, still mostly looking at the floor.

"What do you mean?" Geeta asked.

"She's enhanced," Scout said.

"An assassin," Daisy said, finally raising her chin. "Built and trained by Shi Jian. But I am not one of hers. Not anymore."

"I can promise you that," Scout said earnestly.

Geeta and Seeta exchanged a glance. Then Geeta turned back to Daisy with a frown. "You saved Scout's life?"

"From Shi Jian's assassins," Scout said. "And from Shi Jian herself."

"That was a joint effort," Daisy said. The corner of her mouth looked like she wanted to smile, but couldn't quite bring it off.

No one spoke for a long moment. The soft sound of Emilie keying her way through something on her tablet only made the silence more pronounced. Geeta kept looking like she wanted to speak, but couldn't find the words.

At last, it was Seeta who spoke. "If Scout trusts you, that's good enough for me."

"Thank you," Daisy said. "I know what you've been through. I wish Scout and I had kept Shi Jian's arm. We could have given it to you as a token."

"You took her arm?" Geeta asked, nearly choking on the piece of bread she had been picking at.

"I'm sure she has a new one by now," Scout said.

"And is madder than ever," Daisy added.

"In both senses of the term," Scout said. They exchanged a tired sort of smile.

"But she's here now?" Daisy asked.

"No, not here," Emilie said, coming back to the table with her tablet in her hands. "I'm not even sure if she's on Amatheon. But she is involved in all of this."

"We already knew she was," Scout said with a frown.

"No, not like this," Emilie said. "Sparrow told us what the governor told you this morning, about the war. I've been reading messages back and forth between the Months and a bunch of other people for weeks now, but it was all in code. None of it made a lick of sense. Until Sparrow said the word 'war.'"

"So what is going on?" Scout asked.

"We already knew the Months were influencing the Space Farers, and we suspected they were controlling the rebels as well, right?" Emilie said. "But I intercepted some messages that were directed to some of the merchants that serve on the council of the so-called governor. They've been there for years, and the Months have been calling the shots for at least that long."

"The governor says he suspected one or two, but he knows it's all of them now," Scout said.

"So, Space Farers, Planet Dwellers, and rebels—a three-way war, but where all three sides are being secretly commanded by the same two sisters?" Daisy frowned.

"Actually," Geeta said slowly, then looked at Emilie.

"The people in the black not-uniforms are the ones influencing upper management," Emilie said. "I don't know who they work for, but it's not the Months."

"I thought it was Bo," Scout said. "Now I'm thinking it was, but only at first. Then Shi Jian stopped relaying his orders and started issuing her own instead."

"But that leaves us in the same place," Daisy said. "All three factions being controlled through one person or intermediaries of the same person: Shi Jian. Why?"

"The Months would see everything burn just because they can't have it," Scout guessed. "They've been dragging out this legal battle for years, but I'm guessing their lawyers told them they weren't likely to win. If they can't have Amatheon for themselves, they'll destroy it."

"But why?" Seeta asked.

"Who knows," Emilie said, spinning a finger around her temple. "Knowing why isn't going to help us, so let's not focus on that now. And figuring out who Shi Jian is and who she works for is really a whole other matter. She's covered her tracks really, really well. So let's just focus on what's in front of us. We see the steps that will lead to war. We have to stop them from happening."

"Sparrow has told us your plan," Geeta said.

"Most of that plan was Sparrow's," Scout said, and Sparrow beamed.

"We're leaving tonight?" Seeta asked.

"We have a ship ready and waiting," Scout said. "My dogs are already there."

"Tonight," Emilie repeated with a frown.

"What's the problem?" Scout asked.

"She's been digging into this Shi Jian stuff," Geeta said.

"But you said we had to focus on *not* her," Scout said.

"I know, it's just hard to get good info on her," Emilie said. "She's planted a lot of false records. It feels like I'm close. But I won't have access at all back home."

"Didn't Bo Tajaki contact you?" Scout asked. "I told him to. He's been investigating the exact same thing."

"Our hosts became a lot less accommodating once we got here," Geeta said.

"They brought me back," Seeta said.

"Yes, they did that," Geeta grudgingly agreed. "But we've been prisoners, not guests. Prisoners they frequently seem to forget about entirely. We already testified for the court. Remotely, from here—we didn't even get to go to the building. Since then, nothing. Not a word. No hint as to when we'll get home."

"Now," Scout said. "We're going home now."

Emilie made a sound of protest, and Scout turned to look her in the eye. "Do you really think if you stay here and keep digging that you'll find anything useful? Or will you just burn a lot more time chasing phantoms?"

"We need you, Emilie," Seeta said when Emilie sullenly refused to reply.

"Fine," Emilie agreed. "You're right. I'll be more use back home. Let down by the tech, but I guess of more use."

"But I'll be more use here," Sparrow announced.

"Is that safe?" Daisy asked.

"Perfectly," Sparrow said. "And I'll be leaving when their ship departs, so we won't even be far apart from each other for very long. You might still need someone on the inside when we're back at

Amatheon."

"If you're sure they don't suspect you," Scout said.

"And that they won't suspect you had a part in us escaping," Emilie added.

"That thing you did to spoof the security systems? I could never do a thing like that. Once they discover it, they'll never even suspect me," Sparrow said.

"I hope so," Scout said. "Are you really, really sure? We have enough room for you on the ship. You don't have to do this alone."

"I'm sure," Sparrow said. "And I'm not alone. I have other friends in the compound and on the ship. I'll be okay. But you guys should go."

"How are we escaping?" Geeta asked.

"By glider," Daisy said, unslinging the cylinder from her back and taking out one for each of them. She snapped hers open to demonstrate the wings. Geeta and Emilie looked intrigued, Geeta almost excited, but Seeta looked like she wanted to be ill.

"It's easier than it looks, once you're off the island," Scout promised her.

"But how do we get off the island?" Seeta asked.

"Back the way we came," Daisy said.

"There's a grate on the bottom of the island," Scout explained. "You'll just jump down, and the glider will catch you."

"That sounds doable," Seeta agreed, taking one of the gilders and running her fingertips over the delicate plastic supports.

"Do we need to finish off this food before—" Scout started to say when the sudden wail of loud alarms drowned her out.

Sparrow's face went pale. She said something, but her words were lost in the shriek of the alarms. She bit her lip, looking unsure of what to do. But then she raised her arms, herding them all out into the garden.

Scout skidded to a halt, amazed by the immense dome of sky that hung over the garden. It was deepest indigo, like no sky she had ever seen, and filled with a depth of stars.

Fake. It had to be. The sky here was always pink.

The sound of the alarm was no less shrill here, even though it looked as though they were outdoors. Sparrow pointed to the lowest part of the wall and Daisy ran up it, leaping and putting a foot on the rim of one of the gigantic planters, then reaching up and catching the edge of the wall and pulling herself up to sit on it. She quickly found a fine rope in one of her pockets and lowered it down to the grass.

Geeta climbed up after, then turned to help her sister manage the last meter. Emilie came up next.

Scout turned to try to speak to Sparrow one last time, then saw the heavy door swinging open behind her. She tried to push the last of the gliders into Sparrow's hands, but Sparrow wouldn't take it.

Then the door was fully open, the guards looking first to the beds and then to the table before turning their attention to the garden.

Scout gave the loudest, angriest yell her throat could muster, swinging the glider with both hands to strike Sparrow as hard as she could. The flimsy plastic exploded into a cascade of tiny pieces, and Sparrow was quite unhurt.

But Sparrow was also clever. She fell to the ground as if knocked over by the blow and lay there as if unable to move as Scout climbed up after the others.

Scout found she could see the sky beyond the wall, but it was like looking through thick, dark glass. Everything was tinged a murky blue. She searched until she caught sight of her friends. Daisy was circling nearby in her glider, hovering like a mother bird as Geeta and Seeta made their first struggling attempts to work out how to use the wings.

Emilie had waited for Scout. She gave Scout one of her signature wide grins.

"Ready to jump?" she asked. From the top of the wall, she could just be heard over the cacophony below.

"Together," Scout said, ignoring the wail of alarms behind her and the sound of feet pounding towards her.

"Go!" she and Emilie cried together, and they jumped, bursting past the deep blue field of stars and out into the rosy pink void.

12

THE CLOUDS CLOSED in around them as if somehow ordered to by the Months. Scout had intended to fly over to where Daisy was circling around Seeta and Geeta, but they had vanished from sight.

She tried to stay close to Emilie's side, but she couldn't get too close, not with as much wobbling as Emilie was doing as she worked out the mechanics of flight. Wisps of cloud intruded between them, sometimes obscuring Emilie's form to a mere hint of a shadow, but Scout never totally lost sight of her.

A cold wind rose up as suddenly as the cloud bank had and chased the thick moisture away. Scout first looked to Emilie, a little below and to her left. Then she found Daisy and the others up ahead, far enough ahead that her glasses adjusted a bit to bring them into detail.

Then she looked back and saw guards spilling out of the Months' compound like wasps forming an attack swarm.

There were so many of them. Where had they been hiding?

The fastest way to the port was across the center of the Galactic Central cloud, which was bringing them close to the two main islands and the marketplace bridge. When Scout focused her eyes forward again to see if Daisy had noticed their pursuit, she saw that Daisy was, in fact, leading Seeta and Geeta closer to the city. The skies here were dotted with more kids with gliders, circling in lazy groups or zipping around in makeshift races. Was Daisy hoping for cover?

Then more figures boiled up from the streets and alleys of the marketplace, leaping off rooftops or the sides of the bridge to launch themselves up into the sky.

Figures in black. Scout's heart skipped a beat in fear that the Months had somehow outflanked them. Had Sparrow betrayed them?

But no, these were Sparrow's minions, and they were flying all around Daisy, Seeta, and Geeta.

They closed in so tight of a formation that Scout could no longer see her friends, just a sea of black figures dangling from black gliders.

Then Daisy suddenly erupted from the scrum, zooming past Scout, back the way they had come, so quickly there was no chance to shout out a word to her.

She had fired another rocket, and now she was charging directly at their pursuers.

The Months' guards were not the best of fliers, losing control of their gliders and tumbling out of the sky as they tried too enthusiastically to get out of Daisy's way.

Daisy banked and came back up alongside Scout and Emilie.

"She's getting the hang of it," Daisy said to Scout, pointing with her chin back at Emilie. Emilie had a look of intense focus on her face, but all that focus was paying off. Scout hadn't flown half so smoothly her first few tries.

"They'll regroup," Scout said, then looked back over her shoulder. "Are regrouping."

"We can't lose them in the sky," Daisy said. "Not even with the kids' help. Let's land in the marketplace and lose them in the crowds."

"Got it," Scout said. Then Daisy caught an updraft and rode it high into the air, diving back down to where Seeta and Geeta were flying in a thick hive of protective gliders.

"We're going to land," Scout called to Emilie.

"How does that work?" Emilie asked.

"We're going to the far side of the bridge. There's an open plaza there with a fountain; that's the largest open space on these two islands. It will still be crowded with people, but unlike buildings, they'll probably get out of the way when they see you coming."

"Okay," Emilie said, her eyes scanning until Scout could tell she had spotted the landmark. "Then what? Just put my feet down?"

"The bridge has gravity. Once you're in the field, it will be hard not to land," Scout told her. "I'll go first if you like?"

Emilie gave a tight nod, and Scout banked around, circling the plaza once before dropping low. Her circle took her in and out of the gravity field, sort of like when she used to pump her brakes on her bike to keep from skidding.

When she was nearly low enough to touch the ground, she got her feet under her and folded her wings against her side. She landed in a run that she quickly slowed to a walk, then stopped to watch Emilie coming down behind her.

Emilie's feet touched and ran; then she was back up in the air. She dropped low enough to touch and run again, but another breeze picked her up.

"Fold your wings!" Scout called out to her.

This time Emilie landed in more of a stumble than a run, but Scout rushed forward to catch her before she could fall to the unforgiving flagstones.

"Nice," Scout said.

"Shame we can't stay," Emilie said with a manic grin. "This was just getting fun."

"Fold it up like this," Scout said, demonstrating by transforming her own glider back into a walking stick. "We're going to need it again."

Emilie managed it on the first try, even giving the stick a little juggling twirl on the end.

And, of course, she had that big grin on her face.

Scout's answering smile froze on her face as she saw the Months' guards spiraling out of the sky all around them.

"Come on," Scout said, giving Emilie's sleeve a tug and then running through the public house archways into the marketplace proper.

"What about the others?" Emilie asked as she ran beside her.

"We'll have to find each other later," Scout said. "Through here." She led the way between two of the shops, a gap in the buildings that was not really even an alley. They had to turn their shoulders sideways to get through.

The space behind was a bit wider, but still not truly an alley, as there was no way in or out. And yet someone had been here in the past, to judge by the piles of discarded trash and the faint scent of old urine.

"They're still coming," Emilie said as Scout looked around and found a gutter to scale up to the shop roofs. Emilie came up behind her, and they both squatted low, watching their pursuers scour the space.

None of them looked up, and Scout was just about to release her long-held breath when one of them consulted something on her wrist, then pointed directly up at Emilie.

Scout and Emilie scrambled back from the edge, then got to their feet and ran from rooftop to rooftop.

They reached the taller shops, the one with owners who lived on the second floor. Scout hopped over the railing to a private balcony, Emilie close behind her. Then she vaulted over the edge, dangling from her fingertips for a moment before dropping to the crowded street below.

Emilie dropped down beside her and, without a word, they started walking, blending in with the crowd. In the usual way that Scout didn't want to ask too much about, Emilie started acquiring things: a gray hat to cover her hair, a festoon of ribbons to adorn the end of her staff. Scout dug through her own pockets, wrapping a blue scarf over her own hair and leaving it to dangle around her shoulders.

From above, anyway, they might be easy to miss in the crowd.

"They knew where you were," Scout said in a whisper.

"I was afraid of that," Emilie said. "I was fairly certain they had put a tracker in Seeta. I wasn't so sure about Geeta and me, but I guess there were opportunities."

Scout led Emilie to the end of the main drag of the garment district, then took two lefts so that they were going back the way they had come, but this time through the food courts. It was even more crowded here, the air thick with the smell of frying street food and sticky sweets.

"They're still behind us," Emilie hissed. "Do we run?"

"It seems like they don't want to make a scene," Scout said, glancing back at the guards following them. They were keeping the two of them in sight, but weren't shoving people aside to get to them.

Yet.

"We'll stay in crowds," Scout said. "This way."

She grabbed Emilie's arm and pulled her inside the public house. She stopped just inside, waiting for her glasses to adjust to the low light.

"There you are!" It was Sammy. He grabbed them each by an arm and pulled them down to the lower level and through a narrow doorway to a short hallway that led to the kitchens. He gave them a little push into a corner away from most of the cooking action and was gone as suddenly as he had appeared.

"Who was that?" Emilie asked.

"Friend of Daisy," Scout said, noticing an even smaller door behind a stack of crates. She ducked down into it and was nearly knocked to the ground by a pair of strong arms wrapping around her.

"Scout!" Daisy cried.

"We have a problem," Scout said after quickly ascertaining that Seeta and Geeta were also there in the darkness.

"The public house blocks trackers," Daisy told her.

"But that only buys us a little time," Scout said. "They saw us come in here, and they'll see us leave."

"There's a secret way," Daisy said.

"Of course there is," Scout said, "but we'll pop right back up on their screens when they go out."

"You should leave me here," Seeta said. "I can make them chase me, buy you time to get out of here."

"No," Geeta said.

"Geeta—" Seeta started to say.

"It won't matter," Emilie said. "They were following me, too. Odds are they can track Geeta as well."

"What do we do?" Seeta asked.

"Get the trackers out?" Daisy said, but it was obvious by the uplift of her voice that she wasn't sure how that could be done.

"They're going to find us," Geeta said.

"Sammy will buy us as much time as he can," Daisy said.

"To do what?" Geeta asked.

"Fight them all," Daisy said, making a tight fist.

"No," Scout said. "No, there's got to be another way."

"How are we going to find it?"

Scout felt everyone's eyes on her. She didn't know what to do.

But she knew someone who might.

Scout shut her eyes and scrunched up her entire face, but there were no other options left. "Hello, Teacher," she said.

"Hello, Scout," Warrior said, suddenly appearing among them. Emilie looked up at the AI as if waiting for her to speak. Geeta and Seeta couldn't see her, but they were looking from Scout's face to Emilie's to see if they could read from their expressions what was happening.

"What? What is this?" Daisy asked, reaching out to touch Warrior. Warrior held out her own hand so that Daisy could watch her fingers pass through it.

"It's a teaching AI," Scout said. "Warrior, how do we remove the trackers from Emilie, Seeta, and Geeta?"

"Look at them with your glasses. Can you see the trackers?" Warrior asked.

Scout focused on Emilie, willing her glasses to know what she was searching for. Just when she was about to give up, she saw it, dots like microscopic stars all through her body.

She looked at Seeta and Geeta and saw the same. If anything, Seeta glowed brighter than the other two.

"Do you see?" Scout asked.

"I can now," Daisy said, although Scout had been talking to Warrior.

"Nanites," Warrior said.

"I was hoping it would be something we could dig out with a knife," Emilie grumbled. "How do we get rid of this?"

"I have something," Daisy said, digging through her pockets. "I picked them up from one of the packs on Schneeheim. They used them to wipe out the nanites that let you function in low gravity and little oxygen, remember?" She found what she was looking for and held it out for the others to see: a collection of tiny darts. Darts with some shining liquid stored in their shafts.

"You had extras?" Scout asked.

"You never know what might come in handy," Daisy said. "Will it work?"

She held out the darts to Warrior, who examined them without touching them. "Try it," she said at last.

"That's not reassuring," Emilie said but took the canisters from Daisy's hand. She and the sisters gathered in a huddle to poke themselves with the darts' needle-like tips other under Warrior's watchful eye.

While they were busy with that, Scout turned to Daisy. "You didn't know?"

"How could I?" Daisy asked. "You never showed me."

"Bo gave her to me when I was on his ship. Shi Jian wasn't there when it happened, but she knew later. I guess I told myself if she knew, you knew."

"But I didn't," Daisy said. "You kept this AI a secret. When I think how many times we could have used her help…"

"She did help," Scout said. "When we were scaling the cliff on Schneeheim, and I shot the rope and dropped the assassins back down to the road. She was there, helping me."

"And when I got to the top, she was gone," Daisy said.

Scout bit her lip. Daisy sounded even more hurt than Scout had expected her to be.

"I'm sorry. I don't know why I didn't tell you," Scout said.

"The journey here, when you were too sick to move. I was so scared. I really could have used her advice then," Daisy said.

"You kept secrets too, though," Scout said defensively. "Every day you went off somewhere you wouldn't tell me, doing work you wouldn't tell me about. Under a fake name."

"That's different," Daisy said.

"Is it?" Scout asked.

"Yes," Daisy said. "I didn't tell you about that because I just didn't want to talk about it. I was ashamed."

"Ashamed? Why would you be ashamed?"

"Because it was the only job I could get," Daisy said. "I was built to be an assassin, but that's not a job I will ever do. And everywhere I asked for work, they suggested I would make a fine mercenary or soldier. That's not much different, really. In the end, the owner of the public house would hire me to bounce out unruly patrons, but not to cook or wait tables. Said it would be a waste of my natural talents."

"Oh, Daisy," Scout said, her heart breaking for her friend.

"This isn't all I am," Daisy said, flexing one enhanced arm. It didn't look much different from any other teenager's arm. Not until she flexed it like that and the muscles like steel writhed up to the surface.

"I know it isn't," Scout said. "I'm so sorry. I wish you would have told me. We could have figured out a different way to earn money."

"It wasn't so bad," Daisy said. "Sammy was really kind. I think the manager was hoping I would bust open some heads, make a public lesson or something. Break some bones. But Sammy was showing me techniques he knows to subdue people without hurting them. I didn't learn more than a fraction of what he knows, but it felt so much better. I was making the public house a more pleasant place for the majority of the customers by removing the troublemakers, and no one had to get hurt to do it."

"I'm sorry I didn't tell you about Warrior," Scout said.

"You named her Warrior? After your marshal friend?" Daisy asked.

"Yes," Scout said.

"She's more than an AI to you," Daisy said. "She's like a mentor? Or family?"

Scout chewed her lip while she thought. "I guess I thought she was when it was just the two of us. But it's not the same as having a friend, a real friend. She's been teaching me things while you're working, school stuff, but when I really need someone, I guess that's you."

"Well, me too," Daisy said.

"I'm not much good at this trust and friendship thing," Scout said miserably. "I hope I didn't botch it beyond repair. I've never had friends before I met all of you."

"Me neither," Daisy said. "We'll figure it out together, though. Right?"

Scout gave Daisy a quick hug, then they turned to Warrior.

"Did it work?" Scout asked.

"See for yourself," Emilie said. "My glasses aren't as enhanced as yours."

Daisy and Scout looked all three of them over carefully, even having them turn around and lift their feet, but in the end, they agreed. Every nanite was now gone.

"So, secret exit?" Scout said.

"This way," Daisy said.

And once more, Scout was following her friend further into the darkness.

                                    13

SCOUT EXPECTED the tunnel to end in an opening under the bridge,
but it just kept going on and on, and she realized they must be heading
along the length of the bridge. The passage was narrow, more a
forgotten gap between the massive stones than a purposely built
corridor.

That impression became stronger as the stones to either side started
pressing in closer and closer around them. Once more, Scout was
walking sideways through a space too narrow for her hips and shoulders to pass through straight on.

Then it ended altogether.

"Now what?" Scout asked, her glasses showing her what details
they could ascertain in the total darkness.

"Up," Daisy said and started to climb. Scout saw the irregularly
spaced rungs of a ladder as soon as Daisy had climbed up out of view.

"Can you make it up?" Scout asked Geeta and Seeta, who were
effectively blind.

"The ladder is just here," Emilie said, guiding Geeta's hand to it. She
made slow progress up, having to grope for each new rung. Some of
them were so far apart she had to hike one hip up to sit on the rung she
had a hold of to reach it.

"Seeta, can you do it?" Scout asked. "It's okay if it's too much. Daisy can carry you."

"I'll be fine," Seeta said.

"I'll be right behind you," Emilie promised.

Scout waited alone at the bottom of the ladder, looking back the way they'd come. Her glasses tried to focus on anything that might be lurking behind them, catching on one jutting edge of stone after another. The constant refocusing was giving her vertigo. It wasn't like what she had felt while in the warp field, but it was similar enough to be distinctly unpleasant, and she looked away.

Emilie was now far enough up the ladder for Scout to start her own ascent. She pushed her glider back out of her way and grasped the first rung. Even after the others had all touched it, the rust still crumbled under her hands, grinding into the creases of her palms.

It was several meters to the top, and the space that Emilie and Daisy helped her pull up into was as dark as the space below.

"Where are we?" Scout asked.

"Nearly there," Daisy said, crawling through an almost perfectly square passageway that was too small to stand up in.

But then it took a sharp turn, and there was a pinkish glow at the end of this tunnel.

Scout was never not happy to see the sky, even this one, which never grew bright enough not to be drab despite the rosy tone.

At the end of the tunnel, Scout could hear the sounds of people laughing, talking, shouting, and just generally going about their day. They sounded very close, maybe a meter or two above them, but they were definitely emerging out of the side of the bridge, nearly at the middle point between the two islands.

Kids on gliders swooped and spun all around them. Some of them were Sparrow's gang. Some were just normal kids.

But a different sort of kid caught her eye, and after she spotted one, she saw others.

"Shi Jian's assassins," Scout hissed to Daisy.

"I see them," Daisy said grimly.

"Which means they aren't even trying to hide," Scout said.

"We're going to have to move fast," Daisy said to all of them. "Drop down, catch some air, but stay as close to the underside of the bridge as you can. We'll come out the other side, as close to the far island as possible. You'll have to climb steeply. Then take the straightest shot to the port."

"That's awfully fancy flying for newbies," Emilie said.

"You can handle it," Scout assured her.

"It's going to be tricky," Daisy said. Her tone was measured, but her eyes were telling Scout that the others hadn't taken to flying as readily as Emilie had.

"Trickier still if we're outrunning… did you say Shi Jian's assassins?" Emilie asked. She leaned closer to the opening to peer out at the kids in the sky, but she didn't seem to know which ones to focus on.

"We have to split up," Daisy said after a long moment's thought.

"Three and two again?" Scout asked.

"No," Daisy said. "No. This time, I'm thinking one and four."

"One and four?"

"You have to get them to the ship," Daisy said, squeezing Scout's arm.

"We all have to get to the ship," Scout said.

"We will," Daisy said firmly. "I'm just going to distract them a little while you four get clear."

"How many of them are out there?" Emilie asked.

"Three," Daisy said.

"Just three?" Emilie asked.

"Plus the guards from the Months' compound," Geeta said. "I see more than a dozen of those still out there looking for us."

"They won't matter," Daisy said. "If you fly the way I told you to, you'll give them the slip. They're relying on technology they don't know we just rendered useless. You'll be fine."

"And you?" Scout asked.

"Like your friend said, there's just three," Daisy said with a forced grin.

"We both know three is more than enough," Scout said.

"Look, I've been asking for word about kids like these since I got here," Daisy said. "If they'd arrived before we left the public house just now, I would have heard. These three have more experience with gliders than they do. I'll press that advantage," Daisy said.

"But what if they're not alone?" Scout asked.

"Then I really need to tackle these three," Daisy said. "Because if she is here, I want to know."

"I don't think she can be," Emilie said.

"What do you mean?" Scout asked.

"Her messages with the Months. She can't communicate with them through normal channels. Wherever she is, they don't have a communications relay through warp space. That's really isolated, which means—"

"Really far away," Daisy finished.

"But who knows how fast that ship that picked her up is?" Scout said.

"Time is short," Daisy said, opening her glider and crawling up to the edge of the tunnel. "Shi Jian is here, or she isn't. Either way, I'm going to distract those three and as many of the guards as I can. You three get to the ship."

"And we'll see you there," Geeta prompted her.

"You'll see me there," Daisy promised, then tumbled backward out into the sky, positioning her glider on her back as she fell, then swooping out into the open sky beyond the reach of the gravity field.

"Our turn," Scout said. "Emilie, you go first. Then Geeta, then Seeta. I'll bring up the rear."

"But we don't know where we're going," Seeta pointed out.

"Get across the bottom of the bridge and climb out beyond the other island. Not over it; stay out of its gravity field. Once we're there, I'll take the lead. Ready?"

"As ever," Emilie said, letting Scout help her position her glider as she leaned dangerously far out of the opening.

Then she tumbled forward, rolled, and caught a breeze strong enough to carry her out of sight under the bridge.

Geeta took a less acrobatic approach, launching herself straight out of the opening beyond the bridge's gravity field and getting her wings under her before circling to fly under the bridge.

"Can you copy Geeta's move?" Scout asked Seeta. Seeta nodded, but her face had gone grayish pale, and her teeth were biting down on her lip hard enough to draw blood. "Go," Scout prompted, and Seeta jumped out, spreading her wings wide.

She wobbled, but not so much as to be truly precarious. She banked a wider turn than Geeta had, but in the end, she too passed out of sight under the bridge.

Scout positioned her own glider but paused in the opening, her toes over the edge and her hands ready to push away from the sides. The lazy circles of glider traffic were all chaos now. Daisy was weaving and dodging around the three assassins, who were far better fliers than Daisy had been telling the others to expect.

But not, Scout was certain, better fliers than Daisy had expected them to be. Daisy knew better than anyone not to underestimate the training and enhancements these kids had had.

The other fliers had fled to other parts of the sky, not wanting to risk a crash with these four. Understandable.

But the Months' guards were missing, too.

Scout leaped out of the opening, twisting and catching a draft just below the edge of the bridge's gravity field. It was a strong gust, shooting her across at a speed that would have felt scarily excessive before she had strapped a rocket around her waist.

She shot out from under the bridge and changed her wings' position to climb, up into the sky where her three friends were waiting, banking around in sloppy circles.

Around them was a cloud of kids in black, but this time, those kids had weapons. Mostly garbage being repurposed as projectiles, but the Months' guards were keeping a respectful distance, a few bleeding freely from head wounds. Scout saw one try to draw close again. A bottle came tumbling out to meet him, hitting his skull with an audible crack.

Sparrow's kids were like street kids everywhere Scout had been. They had deadly aim, and no use for warning shots.

Scout rode a current up to a position just over the others and waggled her wings to get their attention. The three started to rise up out of their bubble of protectors, but the guards tried to close in around them.

Scout rolled onto her back and soared awkwardly in the opposite direction.

"Keep going straight on!" she yelled to the others as she passed over their heads. They gaped up at her, and she knew she must look insane. She was barely staying aloft; it was a lot harder to control her mass with the flimsy glider beneath her.

But she had something she needed to do.

When she was close enough, she rolled over again, pulling the gun from the holster at the base of her spine. Another item they had taken from Schneeheim, filled with darts, as the assassins had been told to take Scout alive.

She had stopped gliding and started falling as soon as she retracted her wings to reach for her gun, but she had planned for that. She had enough altitude compared to the others. She took aim and fired, over and over until she was out of darts.

A cheer rose up from the kids around her, and a few of the more eager converged on the few guards that remained after Scout had run out of shots.

"Thanks!" Scout yelled, although she doubted more than a few of the closest could hear her. "And tell Sparrow thanks as well!"

By then she had stowed her gun and was climbing back up into the sky, making for the distant dots that were her friends.

The rest of the trip to the port was no more challenging than the usual flight through the irregular winds and twisting cloud formations that always marked the atmosphere at the edge of the sphere. Scout landed first, then turned to catch the next if they needed help.

Emilie touched down, shutting her wings at once as Scout had, then turned on the opposite side of the jutting rock, reaching out just as Scout was. Geeta stumbled a bit but kept moving forward, getting out of the way before Seeta came down.

Somewhere in the last few minutes, Seeta had gotten the hang of flying. She landed with graceful ease on one tiptoe, folding her wings and bringing the other foot down in a motion that rolled seamlessly into a walk into the port building.

"Where's Daisy?" Emilie asked, scanning the skies with her augmented glasses. They were largely designed for interfacing with computer systems, though, and didn't have the vision adjustment features that Scout had.

"I don't see her," Scout said. "But she'll be here. I'm going to take you three to the ship so you can tell the captain to get ready to go."

"But Daisy," Emilie persisted.

"She'll be here," Scout assured her. "She's tougher than she looks."

Geeta let out a bark of a laugh that almost seemed to take herself by surprise. "Sorry," she said, "but have you *seen* Daisy? Daisy looks like she eats hulking mercenaries for breakfast. Those three little kids don't stand a chance."

"Those three little kids are like Shi Jian," Scout explained as she hurried them across the waiting room to the maze of corridors beyond. "Augmented in every possible way, nearly unkillable, and highly trained in the art of killing."

"But so was she," Emilie said. "Right?"

"She was trained," Scout allowed. "But she never took an assignment. She chose a different path. Killing, that's not her way."

"But it could be," Emilie said. "The moment she chooses to be."

"Stop it, Emilie," Geeta said. "She's on our side."

Scout stopped outside the airlock to Jocquette Dieu-le-Veut's ship. Either the dogs had never stopped barking, or they sensed her presence on the other side of the door.

"They're going to go nuts if they see me and I just leave again," Scout said.

"Leave?" Seeta said.

"I have to get Daisy," Scout said. "As soon as I'm out of sight, get inside. Don't let the dogs slip past you! And tell Jocquette to get ready, because when we get here, we're going to be… is there a word that means more than hurry?"

"We'll convey the sense of it to her," Emilie promised. "Go get your friend."

Scout ran back down the corridor and was unfurling her glider as she crossed the waiting room, preparing to launch into the air before even getting out the doors, when she saw it wasn't necessary.

Daisy was limping her way across the waiting area, dragging the shattered remains of her glider behind her.

"Daisy!" Scout cried.

Daisy looked up, and Scout saw an ugly gash across her forehead, a gash so deep that even through the flood of wrongly colored blood, Scout could see the dull shine of her skull.

Not bone.

"I'm okay," Daisy said, her words slurring together.

"Are they behind you?" Scout asked, catching hold of Daisy before she could fall to the ground and looking over her shoulder for signs of pursuit.

"No, not yet," Daisy said. "They fell back, but they must have come here on a ship."

"Then let's get to our ship and get out of here," Scout said.

Scout slipped an arm around Daisy's waist. Augmented bodies were heavy, and the weight of her made Scout stagger, but she forced her legs to straighten, to support her friend.

Five days to Amatheon. More than enough time for Daisy to heal.

If they could just get to the ship. The distance seemed to have increased exponentially since the last time she had traversed it, and her vision was starting to fade into a cascade of black explosions from the effort of supporting Daisy's weight before they reached the last branching corridor.

Then her knees did buckle underneath her, and she stumbled, Daisy's full weight collapsing on top of her. She was hurt badly, worse than she had let on, and Scout was trapped underneath her.

Then she heard a familiar metallic clanging and looked up to see Captain Jocquette Dieu-le-Veut clomping down the sloping hallway to them. She grasped the back of Daisy's jacket in her metallic hand, then straightened with an odd sort of shuffle.

It must be awkward, having superstrength on mismatched sides of your body.

It must be murder on the back.

But she was managing, throwing Daisy's heavy frame over her shoulders and calling back over her shoulder to Scout.

"Get up off the floor! We have a launch window, and I'm not going to miss it!"

Somehow Scout got her arms underneath her and blinked the

fuzziness out of the edges of her vision. She stumbled up the ramp and through the airlock.

Someone shut the door behind her, and she let herself collapse to the floor.

Where she was immediately tackled by two very ecstatic dogs who quickly bowled her over. When they had communicated the worst of their worry and the best of their excitement at seeing her return, she managed to sit up and hug them tight.

Then she felt the ship detach from the airlock and she hugged them even tighter.

They were going home.

14

SCOUT SPENT most of the journey in the airlock. She wasn't sure if Daisy had ever thought to ask how big of a ship Captain Jocquette Dieu-le-Veut flew, but the fact that she never flew with a crew or passengers besides a single dog might have been a clue that it would be close quarters.

At least the captain had given up her personal bunk space. Geeta and Seeta spent most of their time in there, sitting with their legs crossed across each other's in a tangle that didn't look remotely comfortable but didn't seem to bother either of them in the least. Warrior had told Scout that the word games they were playing were specific cognitive exercises designed to aid in Seeta's recovery.

Scout wondered if Seeta knew that. In the flight to get away from Galactic Central she hadn't needed to talk enough for Scout to notice it, but by the second casual conversation aboard the ship, it became apparent that she was having trouble with word recall. But she showed no frustration; it was like she didn't even notice it.

There was no way to pull Geeta aside to ask her without Seeta overhearing either.

Emilie was tucked up in a communications and navigation nook behind the cockpit. It wasn't even comfortable for sitting in, but in free fall, the tightness of the space mattered less. She spent too much time searching the library records she had downloaded to her node before they entered warp space. But what catnaps she took and what food Geeta gave her to eat must have been more than she had been getting back at Galactic Central, because her appearance started to improve. She looked less like her body was consuming itself to fuel the frantic racings of her mind.

Daisy split her time between the cockpit with Jocquette and the airlock with Scout and the dogs. Scout could see how jumpy she was, and it wasn't hard to guess why. Daisy was an obsessive planner, but there was nothing for her to plan now. When they reached Amatheon, they would be following Sparrow's plan, and whatever modifications Tom Tom had cooked up on his own. They didn't have any intel to base their own planning on.

At least Scout was feeling mostly okay. She could close her eyes, and the feeling of tumbling forward would be there, but like a ghost of its former self. It was easy to ignore. Jocquette's ship wasn't as fast as even the tribunal enforcer ship had been.

Scout hoped this meant she wouldn't be sick later after they left hyperspace. That would be very inconvenient. No one was going to pause their warmongering until she felt better. If it did come up, she'd have to soldier through.

But in the meantime, there was nothing to do but wait, which was worse here than it had been at Galactic Central given the tighter quarters and the lack of anything productive to do.

At least Daisy's wounds were healing. The gash in her head was a jagged scar now, but already fading to silvery faintness. The deep wound in her thigh, the one she hadn't shown Scout until they were in warp space, was only a faint half-moon barely discernible to the rest of her flesh.

It made Scout wonder how many other wounds she had healed from in the past that had disappeared without a trace. And she remembered what Shi Jian said, about how their super senses made the pain more acute for them than for normal people.

The dogs had grown too used to being shuffled about to new locations to make much of a fuss about being back in free fall again.

They remembered all the games Scout had invented to pass the time when she had been stuck waiting in microgravity on Amatheon's moon.

Their favorite was one Scout called Juggle the Dogs, which involved pushing first one and then the other towards a wall. They had learned to change their position and push off the walls to come sailing back to her, and she kept it up as long as she could until the timing fell apart and both dogs collided with her at once. Then it was all laughing, licking, and hugs.

She was playing that game with the dogs when she heard the sound of raised voices from the front of the ship. That was distinctly odd. Even trapped in close quarters with everyone tense and anxious about what they would face when they reached their destination, no one had so much as snapped at each other so far. Now, on the last day of the journey, who was melting down?

Scout caught the dogs and tucked them into their crate, where Emilie had rigged up a water bottle that released droplets when they licked it but didn't leak in the microgravity.

Then she pulled herself out of the airlock, past the latrine behind its accordion door and the even tinier kitchenette, to the space between the communications nook and the captain's bunk.

"What's going on?" Scout asked.

Daisy poked her head out of the cockpit. "I was wondering that myself."

"Look at her," Geeta said from where she was floating, arms and legs crossed in stern disapproval. Scout looked past Geeta to Seeta, but she just gave a sad shake of her head and pointed behind Scout.

Scout pivoted to see Emilie behind her. It took a long moment to realize what Geeta must have gotten upset about.

"Your hair's red again," Scout said. When they had met, Emilie's hair had been a candy-colored shade of red. It had faded while she had been with the Months. "Well, it's different, but nice," Scout said diplomatically.

It was the exact same shade of flame red as Captain Jocquette's.

"I like it," Emilie said as if that ended the matter.

"What's the objection?" Daisy asked.

"What if we have to go incognito?" Geeta asked. "She's a walking target."

"I can wear a hat," Emilie said.

"This wasn't a problem before," Scout said. "You and Seeta had color in your hair as well."

"It faded out," Geeta said.

"And we colored it specifically so we could hide it when we had to," Seeta said, touching the nape of her neck where her purple streak had once been.

"I can hide it with a hat," Emilie said stubbornly. "Besides, when your color faded, you were left with rich locks of inky black hair. I just had… what I had. Ick. It's not me."

"Well, technically—" Geeta started to say, but Daisy cut her off.

"Definitely, this is you," she said. "I just met you, and I can see how this is you. Your whole demeanor is different."

The others all studied Emilie closely, trying to notice what Daisy was talking about. Scout thought she could see it too, but Emilie was clearly getting self-conscious with everyone staring at her.

Then there was a jolt, and Daisy looked back over her shoulder.

"We're back in normal space," she announced, then ducked away to slide into the copilot's seat. Scout moved forward to the cockpit doorway to see out the windows.

She had expected a view of Amatheon filling the screen, or perhaps of *Amatheon Orbiter 1*. But she appeared to be looking out at nothing at all.

"Where are we?" she asked.

"Outside the barricade," the captain said. "You have permission to pass, or what?"

"The barricade is still up?" Scout said. "The court case—"

"Technically hasn't wrapped up yet," Emilie finished for her.

"So, how do we get across it?" Scout asked.

There was a long silence. Then the captain looked up at her.

"You're asking me? This was your gig. I'm just the pilot," she said.

Scout bit back a sharp reply. She was, after all, technically right.

"Can we get a message out to Sparrow's friend? Tom Tom?" Daisy asked.

"Not with my equipment," the captain said. "From what I'm reading, the planet, moon, and all orbiting satellites are on complete lockdown."

"Can you send a message to the tribunal enforcers?" Geeta asked Scout.

"I don't know," Scout said. "There was one among them who was an ally, but did they come back here after taking me to Schneeheim? Did that fulfill their obligation, which was really to the Torreses and not to me? I'm not even sure how to send a message to a specific enforcer. And I'm not sure if they're all our friends."

"Do we have anything else to try?" Daisy asked.

They all floated in silence until Geeta fixed her eyes on Scout.

"I guess not," Scout conceded.

"Dictate your message," Emilie told her, hands flying over the controls on the communications board. "I'll find a way to get it where it needs to go."

Suddenly, the board behind her, the one for navigation, started flashing and beeping loudly.

"What is it?" Scout asked as Emilie spun around.

"There's a ship coming out of warp right on top of us," she said.

"How is that possible?" Geeta asked. "The odds against it are astronomical."

"Unless," Daisy said with a hard edge to her voice, "it's not a coincidence at all."

There was another long silence, broken by Captain Jocquette's slightly self-conscious chuckle.

"You got me," she said, raising her hands as if admitting to cheating at cards.

"We got you doing what?" Daisy demanded.

"It's the Months' ship," Emilie said. "Nothing else I've ever seen has been so brutally boxy."

"The Months," Scout said. "You sold us out to the Months."

"I paid you to be discreet," Daisy said.

"But they paid me more," she said with a shrug.

"Do you even know what they're going to do to us?" Daisy demanded.

"Not my business," the captain said, but then added, "if you're worried about it, I'd be happy to watch the dogs for you. Free of charge."

"I'm not leaving my dogs with you," Scout said from between gritted teeth.

"Suit yourself," the captain said with a shrug. "Although I just might ask the Months about it. Don't know why they would say no, and I did such a good job of getting you all here where they wanted you."

Daisy was seething, hands in fists, but Scout rested a hand on her shoulder and gave a little shake of her head. Nothing they could do to the captain was going to make anything any better.

"We're being towed aboard now," the captain told them, lifting her hands away from the controls as if to emphasize the point. "You might as well line up in the airlock and let them cuff you. No sense in risking injury fighting the inevitable."

"No sense in not doing it either," Daisy hissed, but she let Scout draw her away.

"We need to hold on to the dogs," Scout said to her. "I can't lose them. I just can't."

"I know," Daisy said. "I'll take Gert. They'll have to break both my arms if they want to take her away from me."

"Thank you," Scout said, pulling Shadow's warm body close to her chest. He squirmed at first, but sensed her unease and relaxed against her, reaching up to lick at her chin as if he thought she found that calming.

Geeta and Seeta were holding hands, heads close together as they felt the ship lift up into the belly of the Months' massive vessel. They had made this journey once before.

Emilie walked past them, pausing a moment to touch Shadow's head, then Gert's. The moment they felt the pull of artificial gravity, she planted herself in front of the doors and gave her hair a fierce tousle.

There was a soft clang as the ship settled onto the deck, then the airlock hissed open, and the ramp extended out to the very feet of the crew waiting for them.

"Come down one at a time," the head of the crew said, waving her hand as if they were already taking too much of her time.

Seeta went down first, ignoring the youths on either side of her making threatening jabs at her with shock sticks. Geeta came down after, deliberately making eye contact with each guard aiming a gun at her from a perimeter they had formed around the bottom of the ramp.

Emilie waved for Daisy to pass her, and holding Gert tight, she did. She stopped at the bottom of the ramp and glared at the chief of the crew.

"Hands out so we can cuff you," the woman said, although there was a small gulping sound before she spoke. Daisy's fierce gaze had that effect on people.

"I keep the dog," Daisy said, hugging Gert tighter.

"We have quarters for the dogs," the chief said.

"I don't believe you," Daisy said.

"Captain Jocquette does not get the dogs," Scout said.

The chief's eyebrows went up in surprise. "I didn't even know that was on the table."

"It's not on the table," Scout said. "Not if you want us to go quietly."

"If you want to fight about it, we're up for it," the chief said. "But it's not necessary. I don't know what story the captain has heard, but what I know is that Jun Tajaki is taking the dogs into her personal custody."

"Prove it," Scout said.

"I'm not inclined to. Believe me or don't."

And faster than an eye-blink, she whipped an arm out. It curved like a snake striking, hitting Daisy on the side of the neck before even she could react.

It must have been some sort of paralytic. Daisy's knees buckled, and she dropped Gert. She gasped for breath, face red with exertion, but just managed to arch her body around so that when she finally fell to the ground, she didn't land on Gert.

Then she lay so still Scout couldn't even see her breathing.

Scout clutched Shadow tighter, taking a step back, but came up flush against the front of Jocquette Dieu-le-Veut. The captain put both her hands on Scout's arms and squeezed. Even the flesh hand had a grip like a vise, and Emilie rushed to catch Shadow before she dropped him. The guards with shock sticks were on top of her before she could spin back around and one jabbed her until she screamed, the other snatching Shadow from her arms. His whine of protest was drowned out by Emilie's screams for all ears but Scout's.

The captain hadn't released her and was squeezing ever harder until Scout cried out herself. When the guard with the shock stick slapped the cuffs around her wrists, it was nearly a relief.

By the time they led her down the ramp, both of her dogs were gone, whisked away to some unknown part of a ship she had never seen more than a fraction of.

Lost. They were lost.

And when she was finally thrust into a tiny cell and locked in, she was alone in a dark so absolute even her glasses had nothing to show her.

As frightened and hurt as she was, the strongest feeling crushing her heart was knowing that her dogs were even more frightened. And they needed her.

And there was no way for her to get to them.

15

SCOUT BARELY HAD time to look around and make out the features of the room: a platform the size of a bunk, but with no bedding; an opening in the floor in the corner that was covered with a grate she was really afraid was meant to function as a toilet; and absolutely nothing else. No air vent, no heating duct.

No way to escape.

She was just squatting over the hole in the floor and debating if there was any point in trying to pry it open given that it was too small to be a way out, and that from the very pungent odor it was definitely a toilet, when the door opened behind her and two guards came into the room.

They grabbed her by the arms and jerked her to her feet, then held her there as a third guard took the belt from her hips, the glasses from her eyes, and even her jacket, pants and boots. The jacket they cut off of her rather than remove her cuffs.

Then they left as suddenly as they had appeared.

After that, Scout lost all sense of time. Her eyes couldn't adjust to the dark; there wasn't even the faintest source of light. Not a sound from the outside world penetrated her cell.

At a time far past the point when her stomach had given up on growling and settled into a tight, angry knot, she heard a click. But the door didn't open.

She slipped off the platform and felt around the walls until she found a drawer standing open. It was at waist height, and she was pretty sure it was in the center of the door.

She reached her hand inside the drawer and felt a tube. Running her fingers all over it didn't tell her any more. She twisted the cap off and tried to smell the contents. She thought she smelled something beany, but mostly she smelled the soft metal the tube was made from.

She squeezed a little onto the tip of her finger and tasted it. It was absolutely revolting and clung to her tongue with a fearsome tenacity. It also seemed to suck all the moisture out of her mouth, making her aware of just how thirsty she was.

But there was nothing else in the drawer and no source of water in the room.

What felt like hours later, she got hungry enough to eat the contents of the tube.

She was idly trying to work out a way to drink her own urine, given that she had no vessel to put to the purpose besides the drawer, when she heard the soft click of the drawer closing.

Coincidence, or could they read her thoughts?

She used the hole in the floor with a faint hope that if they were watching her, they'd reward her with water, but the drawer remained closed.

Her stomach rumbled, not liking the contents of the tube.

She drifted in and out of sleep, until she was jolted rudely awake by the loud clang of the door and the sudden piercing brightness of the light beyond.

"Get up," the chief of the guards said to her, yanking her to her feet and thrusting a pair of soft pants at her. "Put these on."

"Am I going somewhere?" Scout asked, but the woman didn't answer.

"Are my dogs okay?" The woman ignored that too, just grabbed Scout by the shoulder and steered her out of the cell.

Scout blinked repeatedly, her eyes slow to adjust to the bright light reflecting off of the metallic walls. She didn't think it was just from her time in the cell. She couldn't remember the last time she had taken her glasses off. At some point, while in Galactic Central, she had fallen into the habit of sleeping with them on. She had gotten used to the way they adjusted to everything for her.

The chief brought her to a very familiar pair of double doors and pushed her inside the audience chamber. Scout stumbled but didn't fall. This seemed to amuse the crowds gathered on both sides of the long central carpet, but she ignored their laughs and jeers.

The Months watched her approach without speaking. Mai appeared as amused as the rest of her court, although she only indulged in half of a smile herself. Jun's face was as surly as ever.

"Where are my dogs?" Scout demanded. She had to shout to be heard over the crowd.

"You ask about them before you ask about your friends?" Mai said.

"Where are they?" Scout said.

"That's not what we brought you here to discuss," Mai said.

"You want a matter to discuss, how about your boss Shi Jian?"

"We don't have a boss," Mai said, her mouth twisting as if the very word was sour.

"She's calling your shots," Scout said.

"She's an advisor only," Mai said with a dismissive wave of her hand.

"But you're holding me captive because she wants you to give me to her, doesn't she?"

"We're holding you captive because you stole from us," Mai said.

"I did not," Scout said.

"You did. You took three guests who were under our care and absconded with them," Mai said.

"That's not theft."

"Where I come from it is," Mai said.

"That's…" But Scout bit her tongue. Mai was trying to bait her into a pointless argument. Engaging in it wasn't going to help Scout accomplish anything. "What do you know about Shi Jian?" Scout asked instead.

"More than you," Mai said.

"Do you know what master she serves? What ends she is trying to accomplish? Where she even is right now? Are you prepared for the consequences when she turns on you like she turned on your cousin, Bo?"

"We were part of the decision for her to part ways with him," Mai said. "We've known her longer than he has."

"Since you were kids?" Scout said disbelievingly.

"Since we were kids," Mai said with a smile. "Would you like to hear all about our history together?"

Scout nodded.

"Well, too bad," Mai said. "That's not what we brought you out for."

"Why did you bring me out?" Scout asked.

"Why, so you could apologize."

"Apologize?"

"For trying to steal from us," Mai said with a sidelong look at her sister, who seemed very eager for that apology.

"I'm not going to do that," Scout said. Her mind was racing, and she looked around at the faces around her, desperate for a clue as to the real reason they had brought her here. It couldn't just be for the theater of it all, could it?

"No apology?" Mai said, arching one brow. "Very well. Put her back in the hole. We'll see if she changes her mind after another ten days."

"Ten days!" Scout cried. "Wait, what do you mean 'another'?"

Mai just smiled as the chief of the guards put a hand on her shoulder to lead her away.

"It hasn't been ten days," Scout said. "It couldn't have been."

But what if it had? What if she was too late to stop the war? What if the rebels had already fired the gun, and the Space Farers had retaliated by taking down the defensive shield and letting the solar radiation reach the surface?

No, it couldn't have been ten days. People couldn't last that long without water.

"Where are my dogs?" Scout said when she saw they were approaching the open door to her cell. The chief said nothing.

Scout planted her feet, refusing to be pushed into the cell. The chief ground to a halt, unable to pull Scout forward. She gave up with a sigh, heading back down the hall the way she'd come.

Then Scout was alone in the hall.

What had just happened?

She looked around, then started running past her cell door, further down the hall.

She was afraid it would be a dead end, but it took a turn, and she took the corner at full speed, running right into the back of a guard carrying a crate of food tubes. He spun away from her.

But not before she had his gun in her hands.

Was this a test? Why was this so easy?

Scout pushed the thoughts out of her mind, focusing on raising the weapon and pointing it at the guard. "Show me the way out of here," she said.

"I can't do that, Scout," he said calmly, although he did raise his hands.

"Yes, you can," Scout said. "Where are my friends?"

"In a different cell block," he said.

"Where are my dogs?" she demanded.

"That I don't know," he said.

"Who does?"

He blinked, as if surprised by the question.

"Does your boss know?" she asked.

"I don't really have a boss…"

Scout growled in frustration and was tempted to shoot one of his knees to see if that got her better answers when she felt a heavy arm slam down over both of hers. The gun clattered to the ground, skittering off into a corner, and Scout found herself encased in a bear hug. She kicked and fought to free herself, but the bear wasn't letting go.

She was carried back to her cell and thrust inside, but she managed to catch her balance and spin around before the door slammed shut.

"Please, my dogs!" she cried, before realizing the person she was pleading with wasn't a guard or even the chief.

It was Jun.

"Please," Scout said again, more softly.

Jun hesitated with one hand on the door. Then she looked away as someone handed her something. She stepped into the cell to set a bottle of water and a bowl of steaming noodles on the edge of the raised platform.

Scout, remembering how immoveable that arm had felt when it had been wrapped around her, decided that trying to attack Jun was not a plan that was going to work.

Then Jun was gone, and Scout was once more alone in the dark.

She tried to be sparing with the water, only taking a sip, but she wolfed down the bowl of noodles.

She was running her fingertips over the interior of the bowl, looking for any last bits of noodle, when the door opened again. Jun looked in at her and gave a little nod as she saw the empty bowl in Scout's hands.

Then she stepped back, and Scout's dogs were charging into the room, leaping up onto the platform to jump all over her.

Scout laughed out loud and tried to hug them both, but they were too excited to sit still. It was several minutes before Scout noticed that the door was still open.

She looked up to see Jun watching her. There was a softness to her face that Scout had never seen before, but she couldn't read the expression.

"Thank you," Scout said.

Jun gave the smallest of nods, then closed the door.

Scout was more confused than ever. But at least she had her dogs.

16

THE ENTIRE CELL was starting to smell like the hole in the corner of the floor. The odor grew at a steady rate, her best way to measure the passage of time. Food tubes came at what she knew were irregular intervals, water even more sparingly.

At least the dogs loved the food tubes. Scout always waited far past the point of hunger and into actual lightheadedness before having any, and every time she regretted giving in. It was like her body could barely digest them.

She was afraid that was the real reason they kept giving them to her.

Scout was lying on the platform, not sleeping. The dogs were tussling together on the floor, and Scout tried to picture it in her head based on the sounds. That was Shadow catching at Gert's ears, that was Gert spinning around and knocking him over with her back end.

The game ended abruptly with both dogs standing stock still, listening.

Then Shadow started to bark, over and over. Gert gave one deep whoof, and Scout was certain something was about to happen. They didn't bark at food tube or water deliveries, so this must be something else.

Someone at the door?

"Come, dogs," Scout called as she sat up on the platform. They leaped up to sit on either side of her, and she wrapped her arms around them, hugging them close.

Scout hadn't heard a thing before the barking, and she didn't hear anything now, but Shadow beside her was a tense mass of clenched muscles, and he was still growling low in his throat.

Then the door was flung open, and Scout turned her face away from the light. She narrowed her eyes to the smallest of slits and tried to look again. She only got a vague sense of a silhouette, someone about her height, probably a boy, wearing a brimmed hat.

Both of the dogs were barking again, and Scout had to catch hold of their collars to keep them up on the platform with her. She was afraid if they bit or just frightened a guard, someone would hurt them in return. But they didn't know that.

The silhouette in the door took a step closer, head swiveling as if they couldn't place her in the darkness of the cell.

"Scout?" he called softly. She knew that voice.

"Tucker," she said.

Then she released her dogs. They both charged at Tucker, possibly only because he was in the doorway and they desperately wanted to be out of the cell. Tucker claimed to have a fear of dogs. Scout would bet anyone would take a step back if they saw Gert charging at them out of the darkness, especially when she had her hackles all raised up like that.

Tucker took more than one step back, but it wasn't enough. Gert jumped and landed with her paws on his chest, knocking him to the floor and sending his hat flying.

Wait—that hat was familiar too.

Scout stepped over Tucker's flailing legs, giving Gert a pat on the head, then bending to pick up the hat.

Her father's bush hat. She had never expected to see that again.

She put it on. She remembered it being bigger.

"Call the dog off!" Tucker said in a furious whisper.

"She's not hurting you," Scout said. Which was technically true, but she was wreaking havoc on his jacket as she used it to drag him across the floor.

"Come on, Scout! How can you be mad? I'm here to rescue you!"

"Like I'm going to believe anything you have to tell me. Particularly here, locked in a cell, the exact same situation I was in the last time you lied to me!" Scout said.

"Keep your voice down!" Tucker hissed, then shrieked as Gert lunged towards his face. Scout caught her collar and dragged her back.

Gert had never bitten anyone who hadn't been attacking Scout at the time. And Scout wasn't entirely sure that the dog didn't judge the mere presence of Tucker as being an attack. She probably sensed Scout's feeling that maybe Tucker deserved to lose a nice chunk of flesh.

But she didn't want that to be on Gert.

"What about the other one?" Tucker asked, slowly lowering the arm he had thrown across his face.

"It looks like he found your bribe," Scout said when she had located Shadow, his head buried in a sack that was resting against the wall near the open door. She let Gert go, and she joined him in tearing the sack apart to better get at the kibble inside.

"I should have led with the bribe," Tucker said, grunting as he sat up.

"Is this another crazy test?" Scout asked, looking up and down the hall. There was no sign of a guard.

"What?"

"You, being here. Mai Tajaki is baiting me again?"

"I don't know what you're talking about," he said.

"Sure you don't," Scout scoffed.

"Honestly. I came here with Sparrow," he said.

"Who told you to wait for me," Sparrow said as she came around the corner. "The part where we have to do this quietly I didn't think I even had to mention."

"We should get out of here," Tucker said, getting to his feet.

"Yes, we should," Sparrow said. Then she looked down at the dogs finishing the last of the kibble. "I'm so glad the dogs were with you. No one knew where they were and I checked everywhere."

"Jun Tajaki brought them to me," Scout said.

Sparrow blinked in surprise at that information.

"Do you know where the others are?" Scout asked as Sparrow unzipped her red hoodie and let two coiled-up leashes spill out.

"Tom Tom is getting Emilie and the sisters now," Sparrow said as Scout clipped the leashes onto the dogs' collars. "Another friend is getting Daisy. We should get to the rendezvous point as quickly as we can. Tom Tom is flying you all out on his ship, but he has to launch before the shift change in navigation. I've bribed a guy not to notice his ship, but he's only on duty for another half hour."

Scout nodded and followed Sparrow's lead through the maze of hallways. She kept to the smaller corridors, avoiding the busier parts of the ship by taking slower, more circuitous routes.

Then they ducked inside what looked like a cabinet but was actually the entrance to a maintenance space squeezed between two walls. When they emerged at the far end of that, they were on a hangar deck. Not the main hangar deck, though. This one was barely large enough for the two ships it contained.

One ship looked like a too-strong gust of wind would collapse it, little more than a cylinder of aluminum with an engine on one end. The other looked like it had been through a war and come out battered and scarred.

"Scout!" Emilie called, waving to her from where she sat with Geeta and Seeta on the ramp to the flimsy-looking ship. Scout let go of the dogs' leashes to give them all a hug.

Then she looked up the ramp to the cramped interior of the ship. "This thing is space worthy?" she asked.

She thought she had kept her voice low, but a girl peeked over the back of the pilot's seat and said, "Perfectly sound, thanks for asking."

"It's not built for atmosphere," Emilie explained. "But we're just hopping over to *Amatheon Orbiter 1*, so it'll be fine."

"You're coming with me," Tom Tom said and pointed his chin at his own ship. "As soon as your friend gets here."

"I'll see what's keeping them," Tucker said and ducked back down the maintenance hall.

"You should get going," Sparrow said to the pilot. "It'll be less suspicious if you don't both go at once."

"Roger that," the girl said, settling back into her seat.

"At least I got to see you before you left," Scout said. "I'm glad you're all okay."

"We'll be in touch once we're back with our friends on the space station and you're with the rebels," Emilie said. "The pilot told me that our people have been in touch with someone on the surface, and I think it's your friend Joelle."

"Sounds like a plan," Scout said. "Stay safe."

"We will. Provided you make sure that gun never fires," Emilie said with a grim smile.

Scout caught hold of both of her dogs and brought them to where Sparrow and Tom Tom were standing behind some sort of blast shield. She watched through a murky window in the shield as the little ship rolled forward towards an opening door.

Then, the very second the door was fully open, the ship started rolling down an infinitely long hallway. The door closed again before Scout could see what was on the other end. She could only assume it was open space.

"Where's Daisy?" she asked Sparrow.

"I'm wondering the same thing," Tom Tom said. "Time's running out."

"Prep the ship," Sparrow said, glancing at a chronometer on her wrist. "If it comes down to it, you'll have to leave without her." She looked up at Scout. "I know you don't want to, but we need at least one of you down there."

"Are you coming too?"

"No, I'll be more useful here with the Months," Sparrow said. "If Daisy doesn't get here in time, I'll watch out for her. Try to keep her hidden, find another way to get her out."

"Thank you, Sparrow," Scout said. "For everything."

"Get on the ship," Sparrow said. "You've only got a minute left."

Tom Tom had already gone on board. Scout led the dogs up the narrow ramp that started at the belly of the ship and ran to the base of the engine.

"There's a crate," Tom Tom said, not looking up from whatever he was doing at the controls but pointing a thumb back over his shoulder to where a crate was strapped down to the floor behind the second row of seats. Scout coaxed the dogs inside, then took the chair across from the crate in the back row where they could see her.

"Strap in," Tom Tom said, and Scout saw the door in front of them starting to open.

"Daisy and Tucker—"

"We can't wait," he said, hand resting on a lever she was sure fired the engine.

The door was fully open, and they were rolling forward when Scout heard a shout.

"They're here!" she said, unstrapping from her seat to turn and look out the still-open ramp.

"They'll have to run," Tom Tom said. "The launch tube is moving us, not me. I have no control."

"You can't slow down or anything?"

He didn't bother to answer, eyes on his instruments. Scout got up from her seat to crouch at the top of the ramp. Tucker was running full out, face beet red and shiny with sweat, but Scout could see that Daisy was pacing herself to not leave him behind.

"Come on!" Scout called, extending a hand out although they were several meters short of the ramp.

And that distance was growing as they picked up speed.

Daisy could see it too. She lunged at Tucker, throwing him over her shoulder as she kicked up to a full sprint. She was nearly close enough to reach the ramp when the distance started to grow again. The ship was moving too fast, even for her.

Daisy rolled Tucker forward into her arms and tossed him up onto the ramp. Scout caught the back of his badly mangled jacket to keep him from rolling back out again, then jerked him out of the way as Daisy put on one last burst of speed, stumbling up onto the ramp.

Scout scrambled to reach the closing mechanism. The ramp snapped shut with an echoing clang and Scout dropped to her knees beside Daisy.

There was a window built into the ramp between them, and through it, Scout saw nothing but stars.

17

SCOUT PUSHED off from the floor, sailing smoothly until her fingertips grasped the back of her seat and she pulled herself into the correct configuration to fasten the restraints.

Daisy managed the same with the smallest of finger-flicks away from the ramp, sliding into her own seat with an easy grace Scout envied.

Tucker, on the other hand, was tumbling end over end in the back of the ship, unable to catch hold of anything.

"Can you push him towards the front?" Tom Tom asked. "His joining me was a bit of a last-minute decision, and I didn't have a chance to explain anything about free fall to him."

"Got it," Daisy said, unbuckling from her seat and catching hold of one of Tucker's feet. "Just lay still," she told him as she towed him to the front of the ship and pushed him down on the seat next to Tom Tom. He tried to fumble with the restraints himself, but she brushed his hands away, making short work of buckling him in before drifting back to her own seat.

"Okay," Tom Tom said. "We're all set. Okay. We're just going to fire the engines and move away from the ship."

"He seems nervous," Daisy murmured to Scout.

"Sparrow's friend is still on duty, right?" Scout asked.

"Oh sure," Tom Tom said. "Sure. Why not?"

Scout double-checked her restraints. It was all she could do.

Tom Tom fired the engine, and they were all pressed back into their chairs. He kept the engine firing, the acceleration building, until the icon for the Months' ship was a tiny speck on his navigation screen. Then Tom Tom gave a whoop that contained so much relief she wanted to retroactively be more worried about their chances of escape.

"How did you get past the barricade?" Scout asked.

"Just flew through it, there and now back again," Tom Tom said.

"The tribunal enforcers must have dropped it," Daisy guessed. "The court case is done. They've found in favor of somebody, and now that person will be in charge of the protection of Amatheon."

"Bo," Scout said. "It had to have been Bo. Otherwise, why are the Months still hanging out beyond the barricade line?"

"Why would they either way?" Daisy wondered. "They're here to make trouble. Why not do it from a closer orbit?"

"They don't want to risk getting tapped by the gun," Tucker guessed. "They can send messages to all parties from anywhere. I'm guessing they only chose to be this close so they could watch."

"Okay, I'm bringing us down through the atmosphere now," Tom Tom said, and Scout saw the black of the sky outside the cockpit take on a lighter edge close to the bottom. The ship began to bump and shake, but nothing like what she had experienced leaving Schneeheim on a rocket-powered airship.

Not that it was pleasant. Scout gripped the arms of her chair and waited for it to end.

At last Tom Tom leveled the ship out, sailing almost soundlessly through the tops of the clouds.

"Are we nearly there?" she asked.

Tucker unbuckled his belt to turn and talk to her. "This is the other continent. A few more minutes. But this part of flying I've done before. We're back in gravity, so you can unbuckle if you want."

"But don't let the dogs out," Tom Tom said. "I don't need that chaos in my cabin."

"My dogs are very well behaved," Scout said, but left them inside their crate.

"Where exactly are we landing?" Daisy asked.

"And do we have a way to get from there to the gun as quickly as possible?" Scout added.

Tucker rested his chin on the hands folded over the headrest of his seat. "We're not landing where we were when I met you," he said. "There's another place that's our actual headquarters, deeper in the mountains. A lot closer to the gun. It's where everyone is. That's where we're going."

"Remote from the cities, I'm guessing," Daisy said.

"Yes, that sort of follows from being in the mountains," Tucker said.

"Daisy was born in the capital," Scout said, although Daisy didn't seem bothered at all by the condescending tone Tucker was giving her.

"Another war orphan?" he guessed.

"Yes, we have that in common," Daisy said.

"You'll fit right in," he said with a grin.

"I'm not joining the rebellion," Daisy said. "I'm here to help Scout stop all that."

"Me too," Tucker said. He didn't seem to mind that hitting Daisy with both barrels of his considerable charm was having no effect on her whatsoever.

"Joelle will be there, then?" Scout asked.

"And Ken and Bente," Tucker said. He was more guarded when looking at her, smiling less and speaking in a more serious tone. "Not Reggie, though. He's been living in the capital lately. Joelle found a distant cousin who would take him in, get him away from all this craziness. Last I heard, he had adopted a pack of dogs and was trying to teach them tricks."

"Good for him," Scout said.

"We should drop in and see him when this is all over," Tucker said. "I mean all of us, of course. Not just you and me. Of course."

"Final approach," Tom Tom said as he started bringing them down over the vast ocean. Scout could just make out the smudge of a land mass ahead of them. They were flying too fast for her to make out details as water became beach became prairie.

Then they reached the mountains, and Scout knew they had to be much farther to the north than she had ever been. Nothing below them was remotely familiar, and she had never seen mountains so big this close up. Not on her home world, anyway.

"Where are we landing?" Daisy asked as Tom Tom guided the ship into a lazy spiral that seemed to center on nothing much at all.

"You'll see it," Tucker said with a grin, "but only when we're right on it. Best we can tell, the Space Farers can't even see us with their best scopes. Not that they'd have any reason to even be looking this way."

"They know about the gun," Scout said.

"Yes, but they only have a vague sense of where it might be," Tucker said. "If they knew exactly where it was, surely they would have dropped a rock on it by now."

"Not necessarily," Scout said, then found herself grasping her armrests again as the ship made a sudden swooping dive that ended so abruptly she thought they must have struck a cliff face.

But Tom Tom was as calm as ever, looking from instruments and screens to what little could be seen through the windows. He was coordinating an entire system of directional rockets with an unconcerned ease. Maybe he was as good as he bragged he was.

Scout felt the landing gear settling on solid ground, but all the windows showed nothing but bare rock. Then he taxied forward until the rock brightly reflecting the noonday sun was replaced by the interior of a cave that had never felt the sun's touch.

"Nice work," Tucker said as Tom Tom killed the engine and unbuckled his own restraints.

"Nothing to it," Tom Tom said.

Scout stood up and looked through the window, but the space beyond was impenetrable darkness.

How she missed her glasses.

"Oh no," she said, suddenly realizing just how much she had lost. "Warrior."

"I don't think they can harm her," Daisy said.

"But I need her," Scout said. "I need my belt and my glasses, but I really, really need her."

"We'll get her back," Daisy promised.

"Not until it's too late," Scout said.

"What are you two talking about?" Tucker asked.

Daisy looked at Scout, who gave a little shake of her head.

"Nothing," Daisy said.

"Suit yourself," he said. "Shall we?"

Tom Tom lowered the ramp, and they stepped out onto the cave floor. It was perfectly level. As Scout's eyes adjusted, she saw that it was bare directly beneath the sun-filled hole in the ceiling, but everywhere more than a few meters from the circle of light looked like a hangar deck. There were a few other ships and shuttles, maintenance and fueling vehicles, equipment stacked against every wall.

"They can't see you from space," Scout said.

"We keep the traffic in and out to a minimum, so there's no reason to think they're noticing any ships going missing over the mountains," Tom Tom said.

Shadow made a plaintive whine and pawed at the sides of the crate. Scout went back up the ramp and lifted her dogs out, catching hold of their leashes.

"Where is everybody?" Daisy asked.

"That's actually a good question," Tucker said. "This isn't the most populous part of the compound by a long shot, but there's usually someone around keeping an eye on things."

"I'm guessing no one was expecting you," Scout said. "Super-secret mission."

"We logged our anticipated arrival time," Tucker said. "We just fudged what the point of the trip was a little bit."

"But only a little," Tom Tom said. "We also picked up another delivery at the same time. I'm going to take care of that; then I'm out of here."

"Sure thing," Tucker said. "And thanks again for letting me ride along, Tom Tom."

Tom Tom sketched a sloppy salute. "Sparrow said she'd be short-handed up there, and it seems like you did help. Almost got left behind, but I guess before that you helped."

Tucker made a sound of protest, but Tom Tom just laughed and went back up the ramp into his ship.

"So what now?" Daisy asked. Scout shared her impatience to get to work stopping the impending battle from happening.

"Let's find Joelle first," Tucker said. "She's probably in the communications room. She doesn't stray far from that most days. Especially now that her brother is gone."

Tucker led the way out of the hanger to a dimly lit corridor. This corridor took a turn, and the next was larger and better lit now that they were far from that hole in the ceiling of the cave.

There was still no sign of other people, but Scout could hear a voice speaking. Then there was a roar of other voices shouting all together, although whatever words they were saying were obscured.

"What's going on?" she asked Tucker in a low whisper.

"I don't know," he whispered back.

"It sounds like someone is making a speech and people are eating it up," Daisy said. Then a darker look spread over her face. "They're talking about the gun. They're going to fire it. Today."

"Today?" Scout repeated.

"How do you know that?" Tucker asked.

Daisy tapped one of her ears. "Enhanced, remember? We better find your friend in a hurry. We're running out of time to stop this."

"Come on," Tucker said, leading the way further down the corridor and down a narrower side passage.

Scout paused before turning down that passage, listening intently to whatever was going on at some point at the end of the wide corridor. She still couldn't make out any words, but the voice sounded familiar.

But that didn't make any sense. Because it sounded like Malcolm Haley giving one of his vicious, fiery speeches—and yet she knew he had descended into even greater madness after the supply of the mood-altering drug he had been taking had been cut off. He couldn't possibly still be in charge. Scout had heard him being removed from command.

But a lot could change in a short amount of time. It had barely been more than a month since she had left, but she felt like an entirely different person now herself.

"Scout," Daisy called, waving for Scout to follow. Tucker had stopped a few meters further on, also waiting for her.

"It's Malcolm, isn't it?" Scout said to him.

"It's complicated," Tucker said.

"Is he better? Now that you don't have drugs to poison him with? Is he getting better?"

Tucker sighed, then walked back to stand in front of her.

"No," he said. "He's not better. And he wasn't supposed to be in charge, but he refused to step down. Since then, he's even gotten worse."

"There's a reason Joelle sent Reggie away," Scout guessed.

"I tried to get her to leave too, but she wouldn't do it. She still thinks she can reach her father, somehow."

"Tucker, I'm going to ask you one question, and by all the stars in the sky, you better not lie to me," Scout said.

"Scout Shannon, I swore I would never lie to you again, and I meant it. I still mean it. I will always mean it," he said with an earnestness that for the life of her she couldn't tell if it was genuine or not.

She glanced at Daisy. Daisy looked at Tucker. Scout wondered what her enhanced eyes could see. Micro-expressions, like the tribunal enforcers? Changes in perspiration or skin temperature or heart rate?

Whatever it was, she had faith that if he were lying, Daisy would know.

"Tucker Hawke," Scout said. "Are you still bringing pharmaceuticals of any kind through any channel to Malcolm?"

"No, I swear it," Tucker said. "And you don't have to trust in my honor to believe that. Because you know me, don't you? You know, the only reason I was doing anything like that was because I thought somehow it would lead to me getting off this backwater planet and out to where the real action is.

"I know now that Malcolm is never going to be my path to that. But you might. That's why I'm not lying now. And that's why you can rely on me to do whatever I have to for you."

Scout looked at Daisy, who was still watching Tucker as he waited for Scout's answer. At last, Daisy made the smallest of nods.

"Okay," Scout said. "I believe you. But Tucker, however you get off this planet, it's never going to be because you're traveling with me. We're not friends."

"I know, I know," Tucker said and resumed leading the way.

Scout didn't need to see the little smirk at the corner of Daisy's mouth to know that last bit had been a lie.

THE SOUND of the rally dimmed a bit as they proceeded down the side corridor, but the roar of approval at whatever Malcolm had just said was like an ocean wave crashing on the shore.

Scout shivered. It was a horrid sound, that many people that excited about killing a bunch of other people. However they were dressing it up, that's what it really was.

"Joelle," Tucker called as he stepped through a doorway into a long, narrow room lined with computer equipment. It looked like it had just been unpacked and set up, crates and spare cables strewn everywhere.

Joelle was sitting at the console directly across from the door. She held up a finger without turning around, speaking in a low voice into the mouthpiece of her headset. Tucker turned to grin at Daisy and Scout; hands buried deep in his pockets as he bounced on his toes.

"Scout!"

Scout looked up to see Ken and Bente crossing the room to see her. Ken caught her hand in both of his and pumped it up and down as he grinned at her. When he stepped back, Scout found herself enfolded in a surprisingly gentle hug from Bente. Bente was built like a bear, and Scout knew from experience what those arms felt like when they weren't being so friendly.

"Tucker said he was bringing you here, but I wasn't quite sure if I believed it," Ken said. "Last we heard, you were heading to Galactic Central."

"I did, but I'm back," Scout said. "This is my friend Daisy. Daisy, this is Ken and Bente, and of course, that's Joelle."

Ken suddenly started whispering, like he hadn't realized Joelle was on a call until just that minute. "She just got a call from *Amatheon Orbiter 1*. I think it's your friends?"

"Really?" Scout said. If that was true, they had gotten set up fast.

Joelle turned halfway around in her seat, but one hand resting on the phone over her ear said she was still listening to whoever was on the line. She gave Scout a nod of greeting.

"Roger that," she said into her microphone. "Contact me again when you know more. I'll keep the line open."

Then she took off the headset and got to her feet.

"Scout Shannon," she said as she walked over. "Tucker said he was going to get you, but I'm not sure I believed him."

"That's what Ken said," Scout said.

"I wasn't lying," Tucker said. "Why does everyone think I'm lying?"

Daisy smirked but covered it with a hand before he noticed.

"It seemed unlikely that if she wanted to get back to us, she'd use you to do it," Joelle said, then raised a questioning eyebrow at Scout.

"The plan had been to come down from *Amatheon Orbiter 1* on Tom Tom's ship," Scout said. "But we got nabbed by the Months on the way. Our friend Sparrow, who works for the Months, got word to Tom Tom and Tucker somehow. I never did hear the story."

"There's not much more to it than that," Tucker said. "Tom Tom got the call while unloading his ship here and I talked my way into going along."

"Before I left, Ken told me he had no idea who was calling your father and giving orders. There was voice and image scrambling. Have you dug into that at all? Any idea who's calling the shots?"

"We can tell it's a woman. That's about it," Joelle said. "Ken has spent a lot of hours digging through the transmissions, but the encryption is too good."

"It could be Mai Tajaki, or it could be Shi Jian," Daisy said. "I'm not sure at this point it matters which."

"At some point it will," Scout said, then sighed. "But you're right. Not now. What's the situation here?"

Joelle groaned aloud and looked up at the ceiling. "It might be easier to start with what you already know?"

"I ran into Governor Smith at Galactic Central. He said he had tried to shut down the gun program some time ago, but that one of the members of his council had continued the work in secret. He didn't discover this until they lost control of the gun. To you all, presumably. The rogue council members are taking orders from… the Months?" She looked at Daisy.

"That was a guess, right?" Daisy said.

"There is a contingent in space that dresses all in black who has been influencing upper management and also disappearing people," Joelle said.

"They were supposed to be working for Bo Tajaki, the cousin of the Months. He's the one who will have charge of Amatheon once the court proceedings are concluded."

"Only at some point, his number one, a woman named Shi Jian, started changing the orders. That's when influencing decisions became disappearing dissidents, and then outright massacres across the station," Daisy said.

"Some of that we know," Joelle said. "Although the uniforms aren't black now. They're green."

"That's good," Scout said brightly.

"How is that good?" Joelle asked.

"It means that Bo still has some influence over them. He orders the color changes for all his employees. We might still be able to wrest them out of Shi Jian's control."

"I don't know," Daisy said. "Maybe it's just their smart clothes he can still control."

"They could disable that if it mattered," Joelle said.

"Or just change to normal clothes," Tucker added.

"Still, I'm going to mention that to our friends in space. If they can convince those employees that Shi Jian doesn't speak for Bo Tajaki, that's a start," Joelle said.

"This rally just now," Scout said. "What's that about?"

"The gun is complete and ready to fire," Joelle said.

"So, when are they planning to fire it?" Scout asked.

"I don't know for sure, but soon," Joelle said. "Things can't go on like this much longer."

"It's getting desperate up in space," Ken said. "Our government has halted all shipments to the space stations. They have some means of producing their own food, but it's limited."

"They're getting hungry," Joelle said. "They can't wait much longer."

"Our mysterious leader ordered us to rob all the supply ships and trains, to maximize the shortage," Ken said.

"So that was part of it," Joelle said. "That was when my father was supposed to be getting medical care, getting better. Two people came down from space to help him get clean. But I don't think that's what they were really there for."

"It could have been all his idea," Tucker said.

"What could have been all his idea?" Scout asked.

"Taking the gun," Joelle said. "Rather than stealing food and supplies, my father took a small team and wrested control of the gun away from the councilor's security detail. It's impossible to steal. It can't be moved from where it's been installed, but we've been sitting on it ever since. And up until now, working around the clock to finish the construction."

"Why did we stop sending food?" Daisy asked. "Was that the governor's decision?"

"Officially, yes," Joelle said. "It's hard to say if he was forced into it or not. But after all the data on those discs you had went public, there was a public uproar."

"Because the Space Farers were inflating their numbers to demand more than their fair share," Scout said.

"Among other things," Joelle said. She leaned past Scout to touch the screen of a console next to the door. "Do you see?" she asked, pointing out a video feed of a network of satellites orbiting low over Amatheon's skies.

"They're all still up there," Scout said.

"For now," Joelle said. "But they've been rigged to blow. With one push of a button, the Space Farers can take them all out at once. And they aren't rigged just to blow. They're rigged to fall."

"Of course they are," Scout said through gritted teeth.

"They said they will only do it if they detect activity coming from the gun," Joelle said.

"Which your father intends to fire," Scout said.

"The gun takes time to power up. Powering up creates an energy signature detectable from space. They'll know we're about to fire and destroy the satellite net before we even get a shot in."

"Will that take out the gun?" Daisy asked.

"Even if they aimed all the satellites for its position, it wouldn't be enough to reach it. It would still fire," Joelle said.

"And from analyzing this video feed and where they placed the explosives, I'm fairly certain they are aimed for the cities and not us," Ken said.

"And the gun is aimed at?"

"*Amatheon Orbiter 1*," Joelle said. "But we've tracked all the stations. There are points when their orbits draw closer together. If we aimed for one of those confluences, we could take out most of the population in space."

"When is the next confluence?" Scout asked.

"Tonight," Ken said. "Then about three weeks from now."

"So that's the point of the rally," Scout said. "Not just celebrating finishing the gun. They're celebrating firing it. Tonight. Because why wait, right?"

"They're willing to sacrifice everyone in all those cities?" Scout asked. She looked at the image of the satellites again. There were more satellites than major cities on Amatheon. They'd be taking out everything.

"We're going to stop this," Tucker said. "It's why you're here."

"How?" Joelle asked.

"Destroying the gun?" Scout suggested.

Joelle laughed a humorless laugh. "Sorry," she said. "You'll understand when you see it. It's so immense all those satellites falling down on it couldn't scratch it. So what are we going to do to it?"

"If we can't destroy it, then we dismantle it," Daisy said. "There's got to be a way."

Joelle opened her mouth, but before she could speak, Tucker, who had been leaning in the doorway, suddenly stood straight up.

"It's your dad," he said. "Closet?"

"You two have to hide," Joelle said, grabbing Scout and Daisy by the arm and guiding them deeper into the long room. "He stops in randomly, but he never stays long. He won't find you. Just stay quiet."

Shadow gave a single bark as if in agreement, and all the blood drained out of Joelle's face.

"We'll be quiet," Scout promised, herding the dogs into the dark interior of the closet.

"If he heard that, I don't know how I'm going to explain it," Joelle mumbled to herself. "Quickly now."

Daisy scooped Gert up into her arms and carried her into the depths of the closet behind Scout and Shadow, and Joelle closed the door with a click that seemed to echo.

Scout sat on the floor so that Shadow could settle himself on her lap. Gert probably didn't register that anything strange was even going on, but she could feel Shadow trembling at being back in a small, dark place again.

Then she heard the sounds of a number of people coming into the communications room, all chattering and scuffling that died out when a heavier set of footprints entered.

"Joelle, all of these are online?" Malcolm asked.

"Yes, Dad," she said. "We're all set."

"Good," he said. "Ken, run through the prechecks for the gun. I expect to see a panel of green lights when I come back here."

"You're firing the gun?" Joelle asked.

"Shortly," Malcolm said. "Call the chief and patch that through to my conference room. Kira and Mitch, with me. The rest of you get back to work."

"This isn't a scheduled call time," Joelle said once the shuffling of people leaving had died down.

"She'll take the call," said a male voice. Scout assumed this was Mitch. She didn't know anyone named Mitch, so why did he sound so familiar?

"Her people get testy about breaches in protocol," Joelle persisted. "What should I tell them if they try to refuse to put me through?"

"Come on, kid! If you tell them we're fixing to fire the gun, they'll patch you through so fast the lines will smoke."

Scout held Shadow tighter, burying her nose in the soft fur of his neck.

That voice had been familiar too, and hearing both of them together, she knew who Kira and Mitch were.

They had been working in the radio watch room when Geeta and Scout had been trying to find Liam on *Amatheon Orbiter 1*. They had been working for the Months. From the one conversation she had overheard, they were in charge of keeping Malcolm doped up and pliable.

And now they were on the surface. If they were the advisors Joelle had mentioned, that meant they had come down from space just to break him out of rehab, capture the gun, and pretend it had all been his idea.

All while getting him most certainly hooked on whatever Galactic Central pharmaceutical they used to manipulate him.

And apparently, they never left his sides.

19

When Joelle opened the closet door, Scout came out, still holding Shadow. Daisy stayed in the closet doorway, holding Gert's leash very near her collar. Her eyes kept darting back to the doorway as if she expected Malcolm to come storming back in there.

"I know who those two are," Scout said. "They work for the Months."

"No surprise there," Joelle said. Then something on her console started to beep, and she ran to plug her headset back in.

"Now what?" Scout asked Tucker.

"I guess Malcolm is asking permission to fire the gun," Tucker guessed. "But personally, I don't think he'll listen if whoever they are says no. This is happening, today. Right now."

"What can we do to stop it?" Scout asked.

Tucker began, "I can take you to the gun—"

But Daisy spoke over him. "What are you looking at?" she asked, leaving the closet to look at the array of screens all facing Ken.

"The call," he said. "Here's the visual. I can give you audio if you're curious."

"No, that," Daisy said, pointing to a screen that just looked like streams of data to Scout.

"That's my program working to find the source of the call," he said.

"But Joelle originated the call," Daisy said.

"There's a protocol in place. She uses a special program that doesn't let her see what she's doing. We don't really know who we're calling or where they are," Ken said.

"You have other recordings, of other messages?" Daisy asked, scanning the data as if she were looking for something specific.

"Tons," Ken said.

"Incriminating?" she asked.

"Oh yeah," Ken said. "The hits on the trains, the stockpiling of supplies, lots of stuff about the construction and seizure of the gun."

"If we could prove who it was, and disseminate that information, would it change things?" Daisy asked.

"I mean, maybe?" Ken said. "It depends."

"Everyone would know we were being swept up into a mess caused not by three conflicting parties but by one person, either Mai Tajaki or Shi Jian," Daisy said.

"This would only prove they're controlling the rebels," Tucker said.

"The rest is much easier to prove," Daisy said. "Give me a couple of hours and a computer terminal, and I can remove the scrambling. We'll see who this is and hear their voice."

"A couple of hours?" Scout repeated. "We can't wait that long. We have to get to the gun."

"No, you don't need me for that," Daisy said. "You can handle it."

"I don't know anything about guns," Scout said. "You do. If I still had my AI, maybe, but on my own? I'm next to useless."

"You're not useless," Daisy said at the same moment as Tucker said, "Never."

Scout bristled as they exchanged a glance, and Daisy gave him a little grin. Great, Tucker's charm had snared her best friend.

"Scout, I have to focus on this," Daisy said. "I'll pull out what I need from the government's systems; those are a piece of cake to get into. Emilie will be doing the same up in orbit. That plus unmasking this person—we need that information."

"The last info dump I brought to the people only made things worse," Scout said.

"You need to go now and disable the gun. I need to make sure that after that's done, no one brings it back online, or drops satellites from space, or does anything without getting to the bottom of every bit of intelligence I'm about to unload on them. They all think they know what's going on, but none of them has the whole picture. And they aren't going to believe us without proof."

Scout sighed and looked to Joelle, who shrugged.

"You should get going," Joelle said. "It's a long walk. Tucker will take you."

"Tucker?" Scout objected.

"Hey," Tucker said.

"My father will notice if I'm gone. Ken and Bente are prepping their consoles to turn over to Mitch and Kira; they also can't be gone. It has to be Tucker," Joelle said.

"Because no one is going to miss Tucker?"

"Not since you left," Tucker said. "I let you escape. He's never forgiven me for that."

"The call is ending," Ken said, and Joelle shooed Daisy, Scout, and the dogs back inside the closet.

The conference room was a lot closer than wherever they had held the rally; Malcolm was in the room the moment the closet door clicked shut.

"What are you doing, Joelle?" he demanded.

"Looking for a spare cable," Joelle said, her voice moving away from the closet door. "I need to set up a remote workstation for—"

"Ken, how's the precheck coming?" Malcolm cut her off.

Scout flinched at the shriek of rage that followed, hugging Shadow tight to keep his whimpers contained.

Daisy dropped to a knee, holding a hand to Gert's head until the low growls quieted.

"What do you mean you just started?!?" Malcolm bellowed. "You're meant to be done by now. Done! Are you deliberately trying to sabotage me? Because you know what we do to traitors."

"Yes, sir," Ken said.

"Do you want to be shot in the back of the head and pitched off the mountain?"

"No, sir," Ken said.

"Because you know what? If you make me order it done, it won't be me that pulls the trigger. It will be Bente. And if she refuses, there will be two bodies to add to the pile at the bottom of the ravine."

"Yes, sir," Ken said. The words sounded muffled, like they had a hard time passing a thickness in Ken's throat. He was holding back a lot of emotions. The trembling quality of his voice said part of it was fear.

Fear, or anger.

Malcolm barked a few more orders and then said, "Mitch and Kira are finishing up another call now. When they get here, I expect they'll find you ready."

Ken didn't bother to answer that time. The loud footsteps faded away down the hall.

Joelle jerked the door open and entered the closet with a stack of equipment that towered over her head. It looked like too much weight for someone her size to carry, unless you saw the bulges of her biceps as she hoisted the stack a little higher.

Daisy let Gert go to help Joelle arrange the components and hurried to connect it all before Mitch and Kira arrived.

"I won't be able to stall the firing sequence," Ken said. They all pretended not to notice the little sniffle that ended that sentence or the shininess of his eyes. "Mitch will be running it. I can't risk it."

"Understood," Scout said. "Daisy will be safe in the closet?"

"No reason for anyone to go in there," Joelle said. "If they should need anything in there, they'll make one of us go get it. She'll be fine."

"Don't worry about me, Scout," Daisy said, still assembling the components into a makeshift computer station without the console to hold it all in the correct positions.

"I've analyzed the gun schematics pretty thoroughly since we got hold of them," Ken said. "I'm downloading my notes to Tucker's wrist communicator. But don't wait for that. Mitch and Kira will be here any minute; you need to be gone."

"Do you want me to take one of the dogs?" Tucker offered.

"Only if you're looking to get eaten," Scout said. But she had to set Shadow on the floor. He moved to stand next to Gert and Scout double-wrapped the leashes around the palm of her hand, just in case of trouble.

"I'll make contact with Emilie and the others," Daisy told her. "Give them an update, see what they know."

"Good," Scout said.

"Best of luck," Daisy said, then shut herself up inside the closet.

There was nothing else left to be done. Scout took a deep breath, then looked to Tucker to lead the way. He gave her one of his best smiles, but when she just glared in return, it faded away until he just nodded, then led the way out of the room and further down the side hall at a brisk walk.

How had it happened? How, after all of her promises to herself, had she ended up once more alone with the boy who had betrayed her?

20

TUCKER LED her through a maze of hallways, ever further from the hangar deck, going down every flight of stairs they passed until at last the final passage ended in an open doorway.

And beyond that open doorway was an immense natural cavern. Turning around, Scout could see the back wall of the compound rising all the way up to the ceiling far above.

The cavern must be put to some use, fully lit as it was. A variety of wheeled vehicles were stored here, although she saw no tire tracks in the sandy cavern floor. If there was a way out that could be driven through, it didn't look like the rebels were using it.

"How did you get all of this here?" Scout asked.

"Train," Tucker said. "Runs from Jakart, past our old compound, past here, and all the way to the next mountain where the gun is."

"The gun is in a different mountain?" Scout asked, panic biting at the edges of her voice.

"Relax, we're catching a ride most of the way," he told her. "It's just through here."

Scout paused to let her dogs find a corner, then whistled for them to follow her across the echoing cavern to a smaller but equally well-lit cave beyond.

It was a natural formation, but not entirely. Scout could see places where the natural cave wanted to be narrower, but someone had chiseled out the rock so that the cave never got narrower or shorter than was necessary to get the largest of those vehicles through it.

Gert and Shadow raced up to walk on either side of her, leashes trailing in the sand behind them, leaving little furrows like snake trails.

"You got everything Ken was sending you?" Scout asked.

"Yeah, it finished a couple of minutes ago," Tucker said. "Here we are."

The cave ended on a concrete platform swept clear of sand. Beyond the platform was an enormous cave, all rounded edges like a worm's tunnel. Scout stepped up to the edge of the platform and saw several sets of train tracks a couple of meters below her.

"You said there was a ride?" she said.

"Over here," Tucker said, leading her to a narrow staircase that ran down to the gravel beside the nearest set of tracks. The staircase was too steep for the dogs and Scout carried Shadow down and set him on the ground before returning to lift Gert up.

"Sure I can't help?" Tucker called up as Scout staggered under the big black dog's considerable weight. She didn't bother to answer, just focused on getting one foot after another planted until she was at the bottom of the stairs again.

She set Gert down and picked up both the leashes, then looked up to find where Tucker had gone.

He was in a vehicle like a single train car left on its own in a separate short line of track.

"Don't you need an engine to pull this?" Scout asked. She didn't have a lot of experience with trains, but she did have some experience with really old Amatheon tech, and this train car looked as old as the rover she had traveled in before she had met Tucker.

That rover had dated back to the first landing on Amatheon. This train couldn't be much newer.

"It works just fine. I've tried it out before," Tucker said.

"Tried it out?" Scout repeated. Tucker grabbed a handrail and pulled himself up, then worked the mechanism to slide the door open. It took a bit of doing; age had settled the frame into a position that clearly preferred that door to remain closed. "I thought you'd been to this gun before."

"Why would you think that?" Tucker asked, extending a hand to help her up. She ignored it, hoisting first Shadow and then Gert up into the train car, then clambering up after under her own strength.

"I don't know," she finally said grumpily. "I got that impression."

"I know how to get there. That's good enough," Tucker said, sliding the door shut with a grunt and turning his attention to the standing console at the front of the car. He looked over all the instruments, then turned a knob.

There was a shriek, and a jerk that sent Scout sprawling on top of her frightened dogs.

And then they were moving. Slowly at first, but ever quicker.

They soon left the light of the train platform behind. The instruments glowed softly, filling the front of the train car with an eerie green light, but all around them was impenetrable darkness.

A darkness filled with rocks, some of which might have shifted, might be blocking the rails.

Might be ready to fall from above.

"How far is it?" Scout asked, desperate to take her mind off of her irrational fears.

"Next mountain over. Should take a few minutes," he said, moving away from the console to sit on the floor next to her. The dogs moved around the car, snuffling in all the corners, eager to find the source of every single smell.

"So, how many places have you been since I saw you last?" Tucker asked.

"Tons," Scout said, patting down her own sides. She wanted to take an inventory, to have every tool and its location fresh in her memory. But without her jacket, belt, and pants, she had no tools.

It was like being naked. That, and staring out into the dark and knowing that if she just had her glasses, she'd be able to see danger before they crashed into it.

"I watched your ship lift off into the sky," he said. "I had a splitting headache and had just gotten reamed at by Malcolm, even worse than Ken did just now. But still, that sight of you rising up into the stars in that silver spaceship—it brought me peace. Not that I didn't wish I could have gone with you. I wish that could have worked out."

"It was never the plan," Scout said, annoyed.

"It got really close to being the plan," he said, but before she could snap at him, he changed his tone. "I know I messed that up. I can't take that back."

"You can never take that back," Scout said.

"I know," Tucker said. "You might not think it, but being stuck here with front-row seats to Malcolm's descent into madness, knowing you were out there seeing all that the galaxy has to offer… that was really hard. I'm not saying it was punishment for what I did, but if it were, it would have been a just one."

Scout wanted to let the matter drop, and he seemed to have nothing more to say. Then, to her surprise, she found herself saying, "I didn't see all that the galaxy has to offer."

"Really," Tucker said.

"I was on *Amatheon Orbiter 1* and nearly died, and I saw one of my friends get thrown as close to death's door as it's possible to come back from. Then I sat on the moon for days waiting to get picked up. Then it was the Months' ship—you've been there. Then Schneeheim, covered with mountains and snow, which might have been pretty if a bunch of assassins weren't trying to kill me the entire time. Of course, I did meet Daisy there. Then Galactic Central. I guess that was cool, too."

"And when this is all over, you'll be going back?"

"I can't think that far into the future," Scout said. A voice in the back of her mind asked her why she wasn't thinking about it, but she shoved it away. "Oh! And I was on a tribunal enforcer ship. Those are transparent, like glass. When you're on one of those, it just looks like you're floating in space."

"Crazy," Tucker said.

Then the train started to slow down.

"Is there light up ahead?" Scout asked, squinting into the darkness in front of the train car. But she saw nothing. "Tell me you brought a light."

"For a trip through a cave? Why would I think of that?" Tucker said.

She turned to glare at him but saw him holding up a bag that he wore slung across his body. "Light, food, water, and various sundries."

"Like tools for getting inside the gun?" Scout asked.

"They just finished the last bit of assembly this morning," he said. "They didn't bring any of the tools back down. Whatever we'll need, it will be there."

"Where, though?" Scout asked, looking out through the front of the car again. Cool cave air was stirring through her hair, making her father's bush hat tremble and the brim flap.

The train lurched to a halt. Scout kept herself steady by grasping the console with both hands, but the dogs were sent tumbling again.

Then they started to rise up into the air.

"What's going on?" Scout asked.

"Must be some kind of elevator," Tucker said. The cave walls around them were suddenly illuminated by a silvery glow from above. He stuck his head out a window to look up, but Scout pulled him back inside before a rocky outcropping could have a go at decapitating him.

"What if there's a guard?" Scout asked. "Do you have a weapon?"

"Not on me," Tucker said. "It's fine. No one is here. I double-checked the crew rosters."

"When?" Scout asked. For that matter, when had he acquired the bag?

"When you were talking to Joelle back in the communication room," Tucker said. "Wow, you really don't notice me most of the time, do you?"

Scout rolled her eyes. Then the roof of the train reached the narrowest point in the cave ceiling and momentarily blocked off all the light.

And then they were in it, the sudden brilliance of it dazzling Scout's eyes again. Man, she wished she had her glasses.

"I guess I don't have to ask where it is," Scout said as she blinked, then stared, blinked, then stared.

The space they were in was hundreds of times the size of the cavern behind the compound below. It was just a little hard to judge that or to appreciate its immensity when a huge steel cylinder dominated the space. It would take twelve train cars linked together to measure its circumference, and most of that looked to be buried in the rock.

How could such a thing be built within a span of years shorter than her lifetime? As far up as she could see, the barrel continued on, all the way up to the dim patch of sunlight that was no more than a shining dot at the very end of the shaft.

"Where do we go now?" Scout asked.

Tucker tapped his wrist communicator and started looking at Ken's notes. "This way," he said, jumping down from the train car and heading to a staircase rudely cut into the stone of the tunnel floor.

"OK guys, you're staying here," Scout told her dogs, looping the leashes through the door handle. "I can't have you wandering around in here. It's too big; I might never find you again."

She couldn't add, even to them, that she was afraid when they left, it was going to be in a hurry.

Scout jogged to the bottom of the staircase, then started climbing after Tucker. She caught up with him with the ease that only comes from daily climbs up much steeper slopes.

"What are we looking for?" Scout asked.

Tucker held up the screen of his wrist communicator. The jumble of white lines on a black background told her nothing.

"Tucker."

"Access hatch," he said, needing to draw a breath between each word. "Should be. About here."

Scout decided he was probably right when the staircase ended in a flat platform flush with the side of the gun barrel. Boxes of tools, half of them sitting open, were scattered around the far side of the platform.

Tucker stopped at the top of the stairs, hands on knees as he waited for his wind to return. Scout brushed past him to get a better look at the gun barrel.

"How are you not dying?" Tucker asked.

"What do you mean?" Scout asked, spotting the releases to remove the access panel. It was almost as big across as the span of her arms, and heavy. She managed to only half drop it on the platform in front of her feet with an echoing clang.

"You just ran up here, all that way," he said, looking back over his shoulder. Scout glanced down and saw the train car a lot farther below than she expected.

"Adrenaline?" she guessed. "This is it. Check it with Ken's notes and schematics. Let's get this done."

Tucker nodded and stumbled forward. Scout stepped back, looking over the toolboxes and noting where things were. Whatever Tucker needed to get this done, she didn't want to have to make him wait while she dug for it.

"This isn't good," Tucker said, a mumble so low she almost didn't catch it.

"What?" Scout asked, eyes still scanning tools.

"This really isn't good," Tucker said. "Actually, this might be insane."

"What are you talking about?" Scout asked, turning to give him her full attention.

"I don't know what schematics they used to put this all together, but there's no way it was the same ones Ken has been studying. Look at this. Nothing matches."

Scout seized his wrist, looking over every line with all the attention to detail she could muster.

Then she looked at the chaos of cables and wires inside the side of the gun barrel.

Her stomach sank and kept sinking as if it were trying to return to the train car without her.

For once, Tucker was being absolutely truthful. There was no way the schematics they had were correct.

Which meant neither of them knew where to start with disabling this gun.

21

SCOUT LOOKED up at the opening at the top of the mountain, just a pinpoint of sunlight growing dimmer by the moment. It was probably just sunset, but the sight was too close to being a metaphor for everything for Scout's liking.

"Nothing makes sense," Tucker muttered mostly to himself. He scrolled through zoomed-in schematic after zoomed-in schematic, each overlaid with scrawls Scout took to be Ken's notes. "Nothing looks like anything. How is that even possible?"

Scout stuck her hands inside the open panel and tried gently pushing aside a neatly bundled mass of cables, but getting a better look didn't make anything clearer.

"We should call Ken," Scout said.

"We can't call Ken," Tucker said. "Mitch will be standing right next to him, watching him closely. It's not like we established a code that would let him tell us what to do while pretending to talk about something else."

Scout frowned, but nodded. He was right. Tucker scrolled through more images while muttering under his breath.

"We should call Daisy," Scout said. "I don't have a communicator, but she's on a computer. Can you reach her?"

"Maybe," Tucker said, swiping away the useless images and tapping at the screen. He sent a message, and they both waited, watching the flashing light in the corner of his wrist screen.

Then text started to fill the screen. THIS IS JOELLE. RECEIVED. WILL GET TO DAISY. SB.

"SB?" Scout said to Tucker.

"Stand by," Tucker said.

Again they waited. Scout rubbed at her arms. It was colder in the cave than she had appreciated while running up the steps, but now that she was still, the sweat on her skin was chilling her.

Tucker's wrist communicator beeped, the sound abruptly cut off when he tapped the screen. "Talk to me," he said.

"I'm here with Daisy," Joelle said, clearly pitching her voice low. "What's the situation?"

"The schematics are no good," Tucker said. "They must have made drastic changes to the design in the last stages. We're looking at the schematics that Scout stole from the governor—" he ignored Scout's slight yelp of protest, "but they must have made modifications since this point. Can you check if they're in the computer system?"

"We don't have time to search all the records," Joelle said. "They're certainly in the encrypted files. Tucker, they're preparing to fire *right now*."

"Can you shoot video?" Scout asked. "Show Daisy what we're looking at?"

"Good idea," said Joelle. Tucker raised his wrist and aimed the top edge of the screen into the open panel.

"Do you see it?" he asked.

"Yes," Daisy said. "The rejiggering was probably deliberate to prevent just what you're trying to do."

"But components are still components," Scout said. "Can't you figure out where they moved the part we needed to take out?"

"It's more than that," Daisy said. "It's likely booby-trapped as well."

Scout, who had been lifting the bundle of cables aside so that Daisy and Joelle could get a better look, snatched her hands back out of the panel.

"Wouldn't a booby trap just destroy what they're trying to protect?" Tucker asked.

"Not if it's something only harmful to humans. Like poison gas or something," Daisy said.

"That doesn't sound like something Malcolm would have done," Tucker said. "It sounds so… without honor."

"I'm inclined to agree," Joelle said, "but what about the people who are really calling the shots? Do we know what they are capable of?"

"Probably exactly this," Tucker sighed.

"What can we do?" Scout asked, desperation starting to creep in the edges of her voice.

She really wished she had Warrior with her. The AI could look inside the panel, find anything hidden away, and tell her how to disarm it.

Tell her how to disable the gun.

But she wasn't there. She was up in space somewhere. Forgotten in a box, or put to other use by the Months.

Or maybe they had erased her very existence. That was certainly within their power.

But the fact was, she was gone, and Scout was on her own.

Well, on her own with Tucker. Who seemed less able to find a step forward than she did.

"You've got to figure something out," Joelle said. "I have to get back out there. The stations and satellites are converging. They will be at optimal configuration in minutes. Do something!"

"But what?" Tucker asked. He had passed from frustration to anger. "What can we do, Joelle? What?"

"You're going to have to think of something," Joelle said. "Because if you don't, those people up in space won't be the only ones dead. Do you understand the energy that this gun emits when it fires? Not just up into space. There's a reason no one is in that cave with you. If you don't stop that gun from firing in the next two minutes, you and Scout and the dogs are going to be nothing more than silhouettes burned into the stone. You will be vaporized. You have to think of something!"

Then the line went dead.

"Great," Tucker grumbled, looking around at the boxes of tools, then up the length of the gun. "Have you got any explosives on you?"

"The Months took all my stuff," Scout said.

"At least you got your hat back," he said.

"It was my father's hat," she said absentmindedly as she examined the panel door itself. Sometimes panels contained helpful diagrams of their contents. This one didn't.

"Then I'm doubly glad you got it back," he said.

"Stop trying to piss me off," Scout said, dumping the closest of the toolboxes over and examining the scattered contents. Beneath the tools was nothing but safety equipment.

"How am I pissing you off? Just by talking?"

"You shouldn't have been wearing my father's hat like it was yours," she said, picking up some of the safety gear. The hard hat was useless. But there was also a breathing mask.

"It was the easiest way to carry it to you," Tucker said. "I didn't think it meant anything. What are you doing?"

Scout had put on the breathing mask, then a pair of thick safety glasses, and was tugging on a pair of extremely thick gloves that went up past her elbows.

"Get down to the dogs," she said to Tucker, her voice muffled by the mask.

"What are you thinking, Scout?" he asked suspiciously.

"If Daisy is right, and this is booby-trapped, only one of us should be standing here. Get down to the dogs," Scout said more firmly.

"This is crazy," Tucker said.

"It's all we have to try," Scout said.

"Then let me do it," Tucker said. "You get to the dogs, and I'll do... whatever it is you think you're doing."

"I'm already wearing everything," Scout said. Then a low hum filled the cave around them, growing in intensity until the rocks around them were vibrating, making the metal supports of the platform under them sing.

"There's no more time!" Scout said as a bluish glow began to spread across the surface of the gunmetal.

Tucker reached out a hand to touch it, then retracted it with a yelp of pain when it zapped him with a flash of light. Scout smelled the faint scent of burned flesh.

"Run!" Scout yelled, then picked up the largest of the hammers scattered over the platform.

Tucker backed up, ran out of platform, and stumbled back down the first few steps of the staircase, but he didn't leave.

"Do it now!" he shouted at her as the hum built to an intensity that made both of Scout's ears ache. The ache was fast becoming acute pain. It felt like her eardrums were going to burst from the pressure in the air around her.

Scout gave a yell that vibrated oddly through the breathing mask, making her sound like a desperate robot.

Then she reached inside the panel with her gloved hands, grabbing and tearing at anything she could reach. She knew she wasn't getting anything crucial, just miscellaneous cables and wires that probably had redundancies built into the system. The blue energy that danced over the gun glowed intensely around her hands, and her gloves started to smoke.

But the moment she had the main board clear, she stepped back, hefting the hammer. She didn't know what function this tool normally served, with its handle longer than her forearm and its massive head. But it served nicely for her current purpose.

She swung as hard as she could, pivoting through her hips and bringing all the muscles of her legs into propelling the swing.

It hit the motherboard with a very satisfying smash. Then Scout's entire world was one intense blast of light, like she was inside the heart of a star.

22

IT FELT LIKE AN ETERNITY, though it couldn't have been more than a fraction of a second. But eventually, Scout worked out that she hadn't just died.

But she might be about to.

Something caught hold of her, and she lurched forward, half running, half nearly falling down the staircase. The blue energy was still crackling up and down the gun barrel, occasionally snapping out and trying to strike her.

The air smelled of burned hair. She hoped it wasn't hers.

She felt a rawness in her throat and realized she was screaming. She could feel her screams vibrating inside her chest, but she couldn't hear a thing. She almost wished her eardrums would burst, just to relieve the pain and the pressure.

The hum was more of a whine now, the blue energy dancing up and down the gun barrel, snapping and exploding like fireworks all over the inside of the mountain.

Scout finally reached the train car and threw herself inside, grabbing both of her panicked dogs near and hugging them close beneath her with everything she had.

Then, nothing.

The pressure eased off her ears. She was pretty sure the dull humming whine she was hearing now was damage to her eardrums and not an actual thing making a sound in the cave, but she couldn't be sure.

She tried to sit up and look at her dogs, poor things with more sensitive ears than hers, when she realized something was lying on top of her and she couldn't get up.

"Get off," Scout said, too loudly but still barely audible in her own ears. She shifted her shoulders and Tucker fell off to lie on his back beside the dogs.

"Sorry," he said. She more read his lips than heard him. "Did we do it?"

Scout straightened up, gave the dogs each a pat, then hopped back out of the train car to look up the length of the barrel.

Nothing looked different. The pinpoint of light was only a faint red now, but that would just mean that the last of the sun was disappearing from the sky.

"It must have worked," Scout said. "We're not dead."

"Unless Joelle only said that to get us moving," Tucker said.

"Or unless she was wrong," Scout said. "No one ever fired this gun before."

"Are you okay?" he asked with deep concern. Scout thought it an odd question, then looked down at the smoking remains of the gloves barely clinging to her arms. She peeled them off carefully, afraid she was in shock and that the first glimpse of charred skin would bring a rush of pain.

But her skin was unmarked.

"I guess so," Scout said, pulling off the glasses and then the mask. "Got lucky."

Tucker grabbed her wrists and turned her hands over to examine both sides, then pushed back her sleeves. Scout didn't especially like him touching her, but at the moment, she didn't feel like pushing him away. They had just survived a thing together, and he was only making sure she was okay. She could allow that much.

"We should get back," Tucker said and climbed back up into the train car. "This is the first place they're going to go when they realize there's a problem."

"Can we get back to the platform before they reach it?" Scout asked. "Otherwise, they'll just see us rushing back and know it was us."

"If we're lucky," Tucker said, already touching the controls to start the elevator taking them down into the train tunnel once more. He looked over at her own hands gripping the edge of the console in anticipation of the lurch that would start their movement down the tracks. "Maybe we spent all our luck."

"We stopped the gun," Scout said. "That was the important thing."

"Your plans just ended here?" he asked. She could tell he was trying to sound like he was teasing her, but the humor just wasn't there. He was as numb as she was.

"We haven't averted the war yet," Scout said. "But if we get caught and… taken out of action, the others can finish the job."

"You've made a lot of friends since you left here," he said.

"I have," Scout said with surprise. "I hadn't really thought about that. I never had friends before. It's a nice feeling to have."

She expected Tucker to say something self-pitying about his own life trapped on Amatheon, his own lack of friends, but he said nothing, just got their train car rolling back towards the compound.

They rode in silence through the darkness, Scout sitting on the floor with Shadow in her lap and Gert pressed close up against her side. She was just noticing the blacks around the train car becoming very dark grays when Tucker said, "Welcoming party."

Scout hugged her dogs, then stood up to stand next to Tucker as the train car rolled up to the platform.

There was a veritable crowd waiting for them. Malcolm stood in the middle of it, flanked by a man and a woman dressed like smugglers in clothes of practical cut but flamboyant colors.

Mitch and Kira, Scout guessed. Mitch's dark hair was shaved close to his pale head, and he was wearing some sort of jewelry that cupped his ear. Kira had her brown hair pulled back in a long braid that reached midway down her thighs.

The train car stopped at the edge of the platform and Scout braced herself, expecting to be ripped out of the vehicle by dozens of hands, but the rebels just waited for her and Tucker to step out.

Tucker tried to grasp her hand, but she pulled it out of his reach, instead unfastening the dogs' leashes from where she had tied them.

But she did step out the same time as Tucker did. She could show that much solidarity.

"What did you do to my gun, boy?" Malcolm asked, his voice low but thick with anger.

"I'm not sure what happened," Tucker said truthfully. "There was a bright light and all this noise, and I thought we were going to die. And then it was all over. Someone messed up a step in assembly, maybe?"

"Not likely," Kira said, fixing her eyes on Scout. Scout pulled her dogs closer. Gert was giving that subsonic growl she did when she thought someone was threatening Scout. Normally that made her feel protected, to know that her dog had her back, but they were woefully outnumbered here.

"She did something," Mitch said. "We told you she'd show up, didn't we?"

Malcolm seemed to notice Scout standing there for the first time. He squinted at her as if not sure if he remembered her, if he had met her in life or in a dream. His frown deepened.

"Scout Shannon," Kira told him, giving Scout a narrow-eyed look. "She's been making trouble for you and for the Months ever since the governor's daughter failed to meet you to make the exchange."

"And Shi Jian," Scout added. "Don't forget her. I've been making all the trouble I can for her, too."

"Don't know her," Malcolm said with certainty. "You, I do."

"What did you do, Scout?" Kira asked. "What component did you remove?"

"I told you," Mitch grumbled. "The only way to disable the gun was to disable the firing daemon in the software. And she's not smart enough to do it."

"Of course she's not smart enough to do that," Kira snapped, and Scout's cheeks heated. It was true she had no idea what they were talking about, but she wasn't dumb.

"The firing daemon was in the firmware installed on the fourth hub," Mitch said. "She must have taken it. She might have it even now in one of her pockets."

"Search her," Malcolm said, stepping back to let four of the rebels come forward—two to hold her arms and two to frisk her, apparently.

Gert's low growl ratcheted up several decibels, and her haunches were pulled all the way up into a fearsome ridge down her back. Shadow snarled, lips curled to show his teeth, tiny but sharp.

"Um," one of the rebels said. None of them were eager to be the first to try touching Scout.

"I'll search her if you like," Tucker said.

"I don't think so, traitor," Malcolm said. He punched that last word hard, as if he knew it carried strong images of bullets in the back of brains and bodies tumbled to the bottom of a ravine.

"Someone has to search her," Kira said.

"Shoot the dogs," Malcolm said.

"No!" Scout said, hurrying to pass the leashes off to Tucker.

Tucker took them from her, but his eyes were wide and showed far too much white. She sometimes thought his dog fear was a put-on. This wasn't one of those times.

"They know you're an ally," Scout whispered to him. "They'll look out for you. Just don't let them go."

Tucker nodded mutely, and Scout turned, stepping far enough away from the dogs that they couldn't reach the rebels who held her arms or the ones that checked all of her pockets and then gave her body an excessively thorough pat down.

"Check him," Malcolm said, and Scout took her dogs back so the same four rebels could give Tucker the same treatment.

"It would have been nice if it had been as easy as pulling something out," Tucker said. "We could've done it and been out of there before the electrical storm started. I think it even singed Scout's hair in the front."

Scout ducked her head to hide the front of her hair behind the brim of her hat.

"She must have damaged something," Mitch said. "If we can figure out what, we can get replacement parts from the Months. We'll have to wait until the next convergence—"

He stopped when Malcolm raised a hand, then closed it into a fist he pressed close to his own forehead. Like the entire world was trying his patience.

Scout couldn't help noticing the way that hand shook. How much were they giving him to keep him under their control? Was there a limit?

Was he reaching it?

"Scout, what did you take?" Kira demanded. "You should know we found your little spy on the Months' ship. She's in our power now. Her well-being hinges on your own actions. Tell me true: what did you remove?"

Scout ducked her head again and squeezed her eyes tightly shut until the urge to cry passed. She couldn't think of Sparrow now, not yet.

"I didn't take anything," Scout said, blinking one last time, then tipping her head back to look Malcolm directly in the eye. "I didn't have to. I just found the largest hammer your crew left lying around, and I smashed every component to atoms. You need replacement parts from the Months? You're going to need to send them a very long list."

Kira swore under her breath, and Mitch threw his hands up in the air.

Malcolm opened his eyes and stared at her for a long minute. Scout forced herself not to look away from those too-wide pupils darting back and forth in random oscillations, in dark irises that looked like they were caught in red webs of burst vessels.

The fist pressed to his forehead opened, but Scout didn't get truly scared until she saw that open hand stop shaking as he drew it back to strike her.

Shadow barked in alarm, and Gert put herself between Scout and Malcolm. She strained at the leash Scout held close to her collar, but Scout wouldn't let her jump on Malcolm. She'd rather take the hit than let Gert bite him. That would surely be the end of Gert.

Then Malcolm shouted a curse at the galaxy at large and turned his back on her. Scout released a breath she hadn't realized she was holding, and Tucker stepped up to stand closer beside her. He gave her an imploring look, but she had no clue what it was he was silently asking her to do.

Or not to do.

"Malcolm," Scout said in her most reasonable voice, putting a calming hand on Gert's head. It took a lot of ear strokes to settle her, but it was made easier when Tucker dropped to a knee to calm Shadow's incessant barking. "It isn't over."

"No, it is not," Malcolm said with a growl.

"I'm not talking about war. Forget about war," Scout said, shooting a look over at Kira. But the woman didn't seem inclined to try to interrupt, so Scout went on. "The rebellion was started to achieve certain goals. Freedom, fairness, safety. I don't know if you had an actual mission statement, but I'm sure you knew in your heart what you were trying to do. And it wasn't revenge for your wife."

"That's all in the past," Malcolm said, but his voice was softening.

"It doesn't have to be," Scout said. "We've reached a point where you can come to the negotiating table and actually be heard. You've given up years of your life for this, years you could've spent keeping your head down and caring for your kids. What good will that sacrifice be if you walk away in a huff now?"

"I don't remember," Malcolm said. "I don't remember."

"I have connections," Scout said. "I know the governor. I know Bo Tajaki, the man who will almost certainly be awarded custodianship of our world when the court reads out its verdict. And, as much as they love being my enemy, I also know the Months."

"Why are you listening to a teenager?" Kira hissed at Malcolm. Malcolm turned back around to look at Scout.

"I'm not listening," he said. "Not yet."

"You seem like you're listening," Kira said, shooting a glare at Mitch that Scout was certain was an accusation of underdosing the rebel leader.

"I'm not listening," Malcolm said again, "yet. The art of negotiation is not so simple as you think, girl."

Scout swallowed hard. "You said yet."

Malcolm sighed as if she were pulling confessions from him. "The governor, this Tajaki fellow—they will seem to agree to anything if they think it means they can get a kid like you out of danger. But the moment it comes time to follow through, they'll have a million reasons why they didn't promise what you think they said they promised. But they'll want to be heroic, for you."

"But not the Months," Scout guessed.

Malcolm licked his lips and gave her a frightening smile. "Indeed, not the Months. If you can contact them and get them to agree to anything at all… well, then we'll just see where you stand."

Scout pretended to think it over; then she gave what she sincerely hoped was a confident nod.

She ignored the wide-eyed look Tucker was giving her. She was not crazy.

23

THE REBELS FORMED a phalanx around Scout to walk her back to the communications room. But it was a pretty loose phalanx, as the dogs were still growling nervously, and none of the rebels wanted to get too close.

Joelle was seated at the same console when they entered the room, but she got up at once to stand with her hand on the back of her chair. She swallowed nervously, and Scout sensed that Joelle was working as hard as she was not to look at the closet door that stood innocuously closed at the end of the room.

Ken and Bente were there as well, but they didn't look up from whatever they were working on, both grouped together in Ken's work-station.

"Joelle," Malcolm said, and his daughter snapped to more rigid attention. "Put a call through to the Months. Scout intends to have words with them."

"Yes, sir," Joelle said and slid back into her seat.

Malcolm turned back to the crowd that had followed him into the room. "You all can disperse. I'll let you know your orders when I have them."

There was a rumbling of acknowledgments, some more enthusiastic than others.

"Me too?" Tucker asked, hovering in the doorway.

"Why would I need you here?" Malcolm muttered, turning away from him.

Tucker looked like he was about to speak, to offer some service, like holding Scout's dogs while she was occupied, but Scout caught his eye and gave a little shake of her head.

He scowled at her, then tried a pleading look. She inclined her head towards Malcolm and shook it again, more firmly than before.

If that didn't work, he was on his own. He shouldn't need her to remind him that he had been branded a traitor and should probably make himself scarce until they were out of this.

They weren't friends, but they were sort of allies. At least, she wasn't anxious to see him dead at the bottom of a ravine. Not that she would tell him that.

"OK, they're putting us through," Joelle said, sliding out of her seat and inviting Scout to take her place with a sweeping gesture. Scout unwound the leashes from her hand, flexing the blood flow back to her numb fingers. Joelle stepped closer to take the leashes from her.

"Good work, whatever you did," she said almost inaudibly.

"We're not out of this yet," Scout said, sliding into the seat. She didn't want to add that smashing that gun was easy compared to what she was about to attempt.

"Scout Shannon," Mai Tajaki said the moment she and her sister filled the screen.

"Mai, Jun," Scout said with a little nod.

"Our scanners are showing that big gun down there as inactive. Could that possibly be your doing?" she asked with dripping sarcasm.

"I hit it with a hammer," Scout said.

Jun smirked, and the corner of Scout's mouth curled up just a bit as she caught the silent sister's eye.

"That sounds ridiculous," Mai said dismissively, and her sister scowled at her.

"It was a very big hammer," Scout said and traded another grin with Jun.

What was she doing? Her allies in the Months' organization were Sparrow's friends.

But they were all out of reach now. They might be few, they might even be many, but they were no one Scout knew, and she had no way to get word to them.

But this thing her gut was doing—telling her that Jun could be an ally—made no sense.

And yet hadn't even Mai told her that Jun was fond of her? And she had given Scout her dogs back. Was that for some other reason than kindness, and perhaps mutual respect?

"I'm not sure why you called me," Mai said, and Scout turned her attention back to the talking sister. "Destroying that gun didn't save us from harm; we were never in its range. So we owe you no favors. And from the sounds of it, it will never fire again, so it's not a threat. Not that it ever was. As I said, we were never in range."

"At least I took the possibility of maximum destruction of all parties off the table," Scout said.

"Did you?" Mai taunted. "Because I'm still in a position to see all the satellites that maintain your protective shield go tumbling out of the sky and wipe out every population center on your dust ball of a world. We have so very many of them, we and can aim them so very precisely. Two people meet to shake hands; there's a satellite ready to take them out."

"At your word," Scout said.

"At my word," Mai agreed with a dark smile.

"Lots of things happen at your say-so, don't they, Mai?" Scout asked.

"Don't use my first name," Mai said, her eyes suddenly cold and angry.

"Bo Tajaki thought he was influencing the upper management in the space stations, swaying their decisions the way he thought they should go, but you always had your own agents up there, capable of undermining anything he did that you didn't like."

"Normal Tajaki trade dynasty protocol," Mai said with a dismissive wave.

"You've bribed all the governor's council members," Scout went on.

"They work for you, not for Tony Smith and not for the people of Amatheon."

"I'm curious why you've called just to tell me things we both know," Mai said. But she didn't sound curious at all, let alone suspicious.

"But it's true," Scout said.

"More or less," Mai said with a shrug.

"And the rebels work for you as well," Scout said. "You've been calling the shots for them, too."

"Who can lead rebels?" Mai said, rolling her eyes. "They're as biddable as cats."

"Normally," Scout said, glancing over at Joelle, who was leaning with her back to the console just out of frame. Scout tipped her head back ever so slightly and made a questioning look.

Joelle looked up, pointing with her chin at someone behind Scout but off to one side, also out of frame.

"Are you alone, Scout?" Mai asked.

"Of course not," Scout said. "You know I don't know the protocols to contact you. I needed help."

"You're with them now," Mai said, eyes scanning the room behind Scout. Scout doubted she could glean much from a couple of inactive workstations. But maybe she recognized the tech.

"With the rebels, yes," Scout said. "The rebels who are under your sway. Because their leader is under your sway."

Mai said nothing, just put one immaculate thumbnail against her lips as she waited for Scout to get to the point.

But Jun was looking very interested indeed.

"He almost got out of your sway, though, didn't he?"

Mai shrugged, still not deigning to speak.

"You had to send two very reluctant agents down here to get him back on the program. The pharmaceutical program. What do you have him on, anyway?" Scout asked.

Mai shrugged again. "We have to keep changing his cocktail. He gets to tolerance levels too fast."

"But they're all mood-altering, right?"

Mai broke out into a wide grin. "Has he been scaring you, Scout? I suppose he would be prone to violent rages. But the main purpose was always to jack up his paranoia. It's easy to get him to believe anything if he's paranoid enough."

Scout glanced over at Joelle, who had a deeply worried look on her face. Scout couldn't help herself. She twisted in her seat to get a better look at Malcolm.

He looked absolutely gobsmacked. Which made no sense to Scout. Had he really had no idea what was happening to him when he took all those drugs? Was he that much out of touch, in denial? Maybe it was a side effect of the drugs, to not notice the effects of the drugs.

"So that's probably going to stop now," Scout said, turning to face the Months once more.

"Whyever would it stop?" Mai asked with feigned innocence.

"Now that he knows, he's not going to keep letting you mess with his brain chemistry," Scout said.

A look of confusion washed over Mai's face, but that quickly turned to rage.

Jun, on the other hand, looked like she was working hard not to laugh out loud.

"That changes nothing," Mai said. "Or maybe it does. Because I'm very eager to drop those satellites now."

"But you won't," Scout said.

"Who says I won't?" Mai said, her voice colder than ever.

"Shi Jian," Scout said. "Shi Jian wants Daisy and me, and she wants us alive. And we're both here, in the path of all those satellites. You can't drop anything."

"You think you're so hard to catch," Mai said. "I've caught you twice before."

"You can try again," Scout said with what she hoped looked like a carefree shrug. "Or we can do it the easy way."

"I don't do anything the easy way," Mai snapped. She leaned forward in her chair, fingertip poised over a button Scout was sure would cut the call. She bit her lip, resisting the urge to beg Mai to hear her out.

If she ended the call, Scout would just have to try again. And again, and again. However many times it took.

But Mai didn't quite touch that button. Her sister had a hold of her wrist. Not tightly, not painfully, just a touch to remind her that Jun was there.

She looked over at Jun, and the two of them shared a silent communion. Scout studied their faces carefully, but she couldn't glean the slightest micro-expression. She had no clue what was passing between them.

Then Mai sat back with a sigh, and Jun slumped back into her own chair with a satisfied smile.

"Fine," Mai said grumpily. "Tell me the easy way."

"You have Sparrow," Scout said.

"I have more than Sparrow," Mai said with another evil grin. "I have all your friends. The Malini sisters and the Tonnelier girl, as well as their clever pilot."

Scout blinked but steeled herself not to react. "Five friends," Scout said.

"Yes, I guess that makes five," Mai said, looking to Jun, who nodded. "Yes, five."

"Five hostages who frankly can't be of that much value to you."

"They're valuable to you," Mai said.

"Indeed," Scout said and swallowed. She could really use a drink of water. Nervousness and so much talking were making her mouth beyond dry. "I offer an exchange," Scout said.

"Five to one isn't quite equitable," Mai said.

"Five to two," Scout clarified and looked up at Joelle. Joelle nodded and slipped away to open the closet door.

Scout didn't turn around in her seat to see Malcolm's expression when Daisy emerged, but Joelle was throwing a lot of nervous looks his way.

Daisy leaned over the back of Scout's chair and waved at the screen.

"Five to two," Mai said.

"Two that Shi Jian wants," Scout said. "That means something, and you know it does."

"Perhaps it's equitable," Mai allowed.

"But there is one more thing," Scout said.

"So many demands today," Mai sighed. "Out with it."

"You talk with Malcolm Haley," Scout said. "Sit down at a table and listen to what he has to say."

"And fulfill his every fondest dream?" Mai asked, rolling her eyes.

"No," Scout said. "Any of that is out of my hands. Apparently, the art of negotiation is beyond my skill set. All I ask is that you agree to sit down with him. The rest is up to him."

Mai sat back in her chair, arms crossed as she thought it over.

Jun leaned over to speak close to her sister's ear. The words were inaudible, but as Scout watched, she knew the sounds those lips were forming.

Shi Jian.

Mai scowled and glared at her sister, but she sat forward to lean into the screen as aggressively as she could.

"Fine," she said. "Noon tomorrow. That open patch of prairie where your galactic marshal friend Liam spirited you away from. Be packed and ready to go. The negotiations will be short."

Then the screen was blank.

Scout turned to face the room. Malcolm had collapsed into a chair, hands pressed over his eyes. Joelle was standing behind him, hands on his shoulders, but lightly, as if she were afraid she'd have to jump away at any moment.

Tucker was still lingering in the doorway, not quite out of sight.

And Daisy was looking at Scout with deep sadness.

"I had to," Scout said.

"I know," Daisy said. "I'm not mad. I'm just afraid."

"Of Shi Jian?" Scout asked.

"No," Daisy said. "Well, maybe I will be later. But for now, I'm just afraid that Mai Tajaki is so angry at being outmaneuvered by you, she's planning to murder all your friends and exchange their corpses for the two of us."

"That won't happen," Scout said.

"How can you be so sure?" Daisy asked.

"Jun," Scout said. "Jun would never let her."

Then she turned away, dropping down to her knees to let her dogs run to her. Because she wasn't sure that her faith in Jun wasn't terribly misplaced, and she didn't want Daisy to read that on her face.

But her gut kept telling her. Jun loved her sister because she was family. But she liked Scout on some other level.

Scout just hoped it was a higher level. In fact, she was banking on it.

24

THE SHUTTLE they took out to the prairie had been designed for shipping things, not people. The back was all one open space with nowhere to sit but the floor, and even that was treacherous given the pilot's penchant for sudden turns and the general choppiness of the air over the mountain range.

Scout had put the dogs back in their crate but was sitting next to them with her fingers through the openings. She couldn't see them, but she could feel Shadow licking her almost continuously. The calmer Gert would occasionally lick at one of her other fingers, as if wondering what Shadow found so fascinating.

Scout grabbed for the little notch in the floor next to her hip as the shuttle dropped like a rock for several seconds before emerging from the air pocket. The notch was designed to tie off cargo, but she could just get her fingers around it to hold herself still.

"It would be smoother if we went straight up out of atmosphere and came down over the prairie," Daisy said.

"In my experience, none of our pilots are open to suggestions from the cargo," Joelle told her. "And that's what we are to them: cargo." Her wrist communicator beeped. Not an incoming call; a reminder.

Daisy reached into the bag she was wearing across her body and handed Joelle a syringe. They were both holding onto straps that hung from the ceiling, but Joelle had to let go of hers to make the walk to the cockpit.

"Hey, Dad," she said, leaning over her father in the copilot's seat. "It's time for your dose."

"I don't need it," Malcolm said grumpily.

"Dad, we talked about this," Joelle said. "It's important to taper, not quit all at once. This is better for you in the long run, I promise."

Malcolm grumbled something unintelligible but rolled up his sleeve so that Joelle could inject the contents of the syringe into his biceps.

Scout didn't know exactly what had happened to Mitch and Kira. She just hoped they were in a cell somewhere and not at the bottom of Malcolm's oft-mentioned ravine.

But she was afraid to ask.

The flight became smoother when the mountains gave way to hills. She could feel the pilot banking and slowing the vessel until they landed. The ramp behind Scout began to lower, and she spun around to see the familiar bright bands of color that marked this particular canyon as unique on her world.

A dark silhouette of a man was waiting, a hand shading his eyes from the midday sun. The ramp settled onto the ground, sending sand and dust scurrying away in little whirlwinds. The man walked halfway up the ramp, then stopped.

Scout looked over her shoulder at Malcolm, who had risen to his feet. He was twisting his hands together, but in the end, he spoke first.

"Arvid."

"Malcolm," Arvid said, taking another step closer until he was fully in the shade of the ship and Scout could see him clearly. Bente's uncle, once Malcolm's right-hand man.

"I'm sorry," Malcolm said, raising his chin as if expecting a blow. "You were right. I was wrong."

Arvid took a moment to digest this, then just nodded. "I have four ready to go."

"Good," Malcolm said with a relieved smile. "Bring them aboard, and we'll get going. It's just a little hop away from here."

Arvid nodded again and leaned back out of the ship to wave for others to follow him.

Scout had been wondering why Malcolm had insisted on only his daughter and the pilot accompanying him and Scout and Daisy to the meet point. She hadn't known they were stopping to pick up Arvid.

Malcolm must be worried that Mitch and Kira had turned people at the main compound against him. He wanted people he could trust.

He was starting to make sensible decisions again. Even if his hands were always shaking when he wasn't twisting them together, clenching them against each other tightly.

Arvid came all the way up into the shuttle, two men and two women trailing up behind him. Scout had never seen them before. Despite the guns they cradled in their arms, they didn't look like mercenaries or soldiers. They looked like farmers about to hunt something down to put in the stewpot.

Once they were on board, the ramp closed up, and the shuttle lifted back up into the air but set down again a few short minutes later.

Scout tried not to dwell on how long it had taken her to walk the distance that first time, with Gert on her back and Shadow in her arms.

It was just as well Tucker wasn't there. She hadn't yet taken him to task for thinking he knew the proper dosage to knock out her dogs. They had nearly died from what he had shot them with. Being back near where she had all but collapsed under the weight of her dogs brought all that anger back, but she swallowed it down. She had other things to focus on than Tucker.

The shuttle settled down in the tall grass, and the ramp lowered once more. Arvid and his people went out first, forming a tight perimeter around the ship and working their way out, flattening the grass as they went.

Scout opened up the crate and unclipped the leashes from the dogs' collars.

They were nervous at first. Gert came out, but only so far as to stand pressed up against Scout's side. Shadow preferred the interior of the crate.

Then a puff of breeze blew up the ramp, carrying with it the dusty smell of dried grass in desperate need of rain. Shadow followed the smell out of the crate, sniffing madly with each step. Then Gert started to sniff, too.

"Go on," Scout said when they looked back at her from the bottom of the ramp. "Have a run."

Gert wagged her tail, but Shadow was already off like a shot, chasing something that had been hiding in the flattened grass. Gert tore off after him.

"They remember home," Daisy said.

"Indeed, they do," Scout said, enjoying lungfuls of the familiar scents herself. "Not much rain lately, I take it."

Daisy smiled. "I might have enhanced senses, but I'm really still a city girl. I'll take your word for it."

"Here they come," Joelle said, pointing into the sky.

There was a glimmer of light that started to streak like a shooting star, and Scout felt a momentary rush of fear. What if they had changed their minds? What if they had put Daisy and Scout in a specific location only to drop one of the satellites on them? They were much more likely to be killed out here on the prairie than under meters of bedrock in the mountain compound.

But the shooting star banked and slowed. It gained form as it drew closer, becoming a shuttle with wide wings like a bird of prey descending on them.

It set down gently just outside the circle of flattened grass. Malcolm came out of the shuttle to stand by Joelle as they all watched the ramp lower to the ground.

A pair of guards stepped out first, leading the four hostages down the ramp to stand blinking in the sun.

Scout could only imagine how blinding it was for them. The pilot had only been in the space stations in orbit around Amatheon. Geeta, Seeta, and Emilie had been to Galactic Central, but as on the Months' ship, the sunlight they would have seen had all been artificial. The stations in orbit reflected the sunlight into parts of the city with mirrors, but it wasn't the same.

They were standing in a world full of sunlight for the first time.

Then the guards herded them off to one side. They were cuffed around their ankles and wrists, and they stumbled as they blindly made their way to stand in the shadow of the Months' shuttle.

Scout had just raised a hand to get their attention when she heard her dogs barking. These weren't hunting barks or warning barks; these were barks of complete joy.

They hadn't seemed to bond closely with the Malini sisters or Emilie, although they had all spent days together in close quarters back on the ship. No, these barks sounded more like their barks of joy when Scout or Daisy returned to the room back in Galactic Central.

The dogs charged across the flattened grass to hop and wag their tails at the bottom of the ramp. Was there another prisoner, someone they knew and liked? Bo, maybe?

Scout had a sinking feeling in her stomach at that thought, but when the feet and then legs coming down the ramp became a whole body in view, she realized it was Jun Tajaki.

And her dogs were jumping all over her, desperate for her attention.

"What's that all about?" Daisy asked Scout.

"They were taken from me on the Months' ship, but Jun gave them back," Scout said. "I didn't know where they were when they weren't with me, but I guess I do now."

"It seems she treated them well," Daisy said, sounding surprised.

"I don't think she's much like her sister," Scout said.

"Don't get carried away," Daisy said. "If she's letting her sister do all the talking and make all the decisions, it's because she's the weaker one in the relationship. She will do whatever Mai tells her to do."

Then Mai came strolling down the ramp. She scowled at her sister, who was down on one knee petting the squirming dogs.

"Dignity, Jun," she said with distaste, then continued her gliding walk across the flattened grass.

Malcolm curled his shaking hands into fists and advanced to meet her. Joelle walked half a step behind him.

Mai stopped and crossed her arms as she regarded the rebels, then Daisy and Scout. She waited for Jun to finally join her before speaking. "You two might as well get on our ship now."

"We're not doing the exchange first," Malcolm said.

Scout felt like something was missing, then realized who she had lost track of. She dipped her head so that the brim of her hat would hide her eyes as she looked all around.

Arvid and his team were nowhere in sight. Scout was certain they weren't gone. They were hiding. With those long guns. She could almost feel them all around her, taking careful aim at the Months.

"I don't think all the formalities are necessary," Mai said. "You'll present your demands; I'll refuse them; then we'll be on our way. So let's just assume we've already done all that and get on with me getting off this waste of a planet."

"That wasn't what we agreed," Malcolm said.

Scout could sense how much work he was putting into not losing his temper. His fists were so tight his forearms were bulging, and Scout thought she saw a small drop of blood fall away from one of them.

"We didn't agree to anything," Mai said.

"No, we did," Scout said. "And it wasn't this."

"Don't get presumptuous," Mai said to her. "Your five little helpers out in the grass are no match for the armaments on our shuttle. I mean, if you want to start a bloodbath, then by all means. Fight me."

"If you won't even discuss dismantling the explosives on all the shield satellites, then Daisy and I aren't going anywhere," Scout said. "Our presence here is this world's only protection."

"You really do think a lot of yourself, don't you?" Mai asked. Her gaze shifted from Scout to Daisy. "You, of all people, must know you're not irreplaceable. Shi Jian made dozens of you. Dozens."

"And yet," Daisy said, "she seems fixated on having me."

"Perhaps we'd be doing her a favor," Mai said. "Breaking an unhealthy addiction. Yes, I think we would be. Guards, put the hostages back on the ship."

"Wait!" Scout and Malcolm called out at once. Mai turned back with an exaggerated smirk on her lips.

But her sister Jun was looking up at the sky, and so was Daisy.

"What is it?" Scout hissed to Daisy.

"I don't know," Daisy said, scanning the cloudless sky. "It's like no sound I've ever heard before. It's like a haunting, unsettling sort of music."

Then Jun pointed wordlessly to the south, and Daisy turned to look in that direction.

A moment later, they all heard it, like a chorus of voices singing notes that didn't fit together at all, over an orchestra of instruments like none Scout had ever heard before, playing chords that bordered on the inaudible.

Both dogs started howling and staggered across the flattened grass to Scout's side.

Then a light shot down out of the sky, hitting a point between the two parked ships. It was too bright to look at, and Scout turned her face away. She could feel heat burning the skin of her cheek, like an instant sunburn.

Then the heat and light were gone, and Shi Jian stood among them.

25

THE FIRST THING Scout noticed was that Shi Jian had two arms. She was still dressed in black, tunic over leggings complete with billowing cape and soft shoes, all except for the sleeve over her right arm. That was a deep red, like drying blood.

Scout thought at first that she must be a holographic projection. She had seen projections she hadn't realized weren't real people until someone tried to touch them.

Then she saw the perspiration just starting to gleam on the woman's forehead and knew that she had to be here, under the sun, in that not remotely climate-appropriate outfit.

Only, how?

"Shi Jian," Mai said with a welcoming smile. "We were just finishing up here."

"We haven't even started," Malcolm said, but she ignored him.

Joelle looked at Scout and then at Daisy. Something in their expressions made that little wrinkle of worry crease between her brows. She took another step back from her father and began furiously tapping at the communicator on her wrist.

Calling for reinforcements? If there were anyone on the planet or in orbit capable of standing up to Shi Jian, they'd never get here in time enough to matter.

"I'm just here for those two," Shi Jian said, pointing at Daisy and Scout. "Then I'll be on my way, and the rest of you can continue with… whatever."

"We're not going with you," Daisy said.

Scout wished she felt as confident as Daisy sounded. She looked up into the sky, but whatever ship Shi Jian had arrived on was nowhere to be seen. Was it hiding in the glare of the midday sun?

Oh, to have her glasses back.

"I wasn't asking," Shi Jian said. She raised her red arm, but whatever gesture she had been about to do, whether merely marking the two of them for removal or initiating some sort of attack, neither Scout nor Daisy wanted to just stand there and watch it happen. Scout dove to hide behind the front landing gear of the rebels' shuttle, hugging her dogs close to her side.

But Daisy charged straight at Shi Jian. She crossed the clearing with inhuman speed and the scream of someone who's already taken one of your arms and is fully prepared to take the other.

Shi Jian watched Daisy charge at her with an unbothered expression. At the last possible moment, she finished raising her arm, palm out, as if asking Daisy to stop.

Daisy didn't. Scout saw the muscles in her enhanced legs bulge as she launched off from the last steps of her run, throwing herself at Shi Jian.

There was another bright flash of light, this time not from the sky but from Shi Jian's open palm, and a crackle of energy that built to a boom of thunder.

Scout peeked around the landing gear to see Daisy lying on the ground, arms wrapped around herself as blue lightning shot all over her body, again and again. Her scream of rage had become one of agony that ended in breathless sobs.

"Yes, it hurts," Shi Jian said. "Especially you. Your body enhances the energy I gave you. It's going to take a bit of time before your internal systems stop boosting it out to all of your nerve endings and then back again." She had bent over as she spoke to look Daisy in the eye, but she straightened now and looked at each one of them in turn. "Anyone else?" She flexed the hand at the end of that red sleeve, forming a tight fist and then splaying the fingers wide.

As if she were reloading.

No one said a word.

"Come out now, Scout," Shi Jian said. "Leave your dogs with these nice people. You won't be needing them where you're going."

"Where's that?" Scout asked to buy for time. Time she could put to no good use; she didn't have a weapon or any means of escape.

"You'll see soon enough," Shi Jian said. "No need for me to speak its name aloud for all to hear. Although even if I did, no one could follow us there. The name means nothing to any of you people."

"Not even the Tajaki sisters?" Scout asked.

"Not even," Shi Jian said.

Daisy's sobs were quieting, but she was making no move to get up. The sight of her lying there at Shi Jian's feet, broken, made Scout's chest hurt.

"My patience runs dry," Shi Jian said sourly.

"Jun," Scout called, still not coming out from what cover the landing gear gave her. "I want Jun to take my dogs." She pulled the leashes out of her pocket and clipped them to the dogs' collars. "I need her to come and get them from me. They're very frightened."

Shi Jian waved a hand dismissively and turned to squat down beside Daisy. She didn't speak, but Scout just knew that her eyes were taunting the still-unmoving Daisy.

Jun glanced at her sister, and at Mai's slight nod, she crossed the clearing to where Scout hid.

"Jun," Scout said when she was close enough to hear a whisper. "Help me."

Jun gave her a puzzled look but held her hand out to take the leashes. Scout got to her feet but pretended to fumble with the leashes, as if they were tangled. She tipped her head so her hat would block her mouth from view and spoke less in a whisper than in a subvocalization.

"I know you can hear me," Scout said. "You're not like your sister. You're more. Like Daisy. Aren't you?"

Jun looked at her, her face a careful blank. She extended her hand again for the leashes.

"Your sister has always lorded it over you," Scout said. "Your younger sister. Because she's always been a talker. And you have a big family, never a moment alone as a kid, never now. But look around, Jun. This is where I grew up. Just me and my dogs, riding over the prairie, only seeing people when we wanted to. Paradise, right?"

Jun blinked. It didn't seem to carry any meaning; Scout pressed on.

"You want that for yourself. I know you do," Scout said. "And you can have it. You just have to stop doing what your sister says. The pirate court, the destruction of societies for fun, that's not your thing. You're about the open prairie, living free and alone, being your own boss of your time and your work."

"What's the holdup?" Shi Jian asked, looking back over her shoulder from where she was still kneeling over Daisy.

"Mai hates dogs, doesn't she?" Scout said as she reluctantly separated the two leashes from each other. "She'll never let you have one. She wanted to kill mine, didn't she? But you wouldn't let her. You chose to give them back to me instead."

A muscle in Jun's jaw stood out as she clenched her jaw.

"Thank you for that," Scout said. "But you know and I know that Shi Jian isn't just going to take Daisy and me and leave. She's going to have more demands for you and your sister. She's going to tell you to kill everyone here because they're witnesses. And she's going to ask you to kill the dogs. And Mai is going to make you do it. All of it.

"Jun, please don't let Shi Jian make you hurt my dogs."

Scout gave the leashes a small tug, and the two dogs stepped up closer, looking with something between curiosity and confusion from Scout to Jun and back. Gert thumped her tail against the ground as Jun looked down at them.

"Please, Jun," Scout said.

There was nothing left to say. She held out the leashes draped over her open palm.

Jun looked at them as if she wasn't sure what they were. She hovered a hand over them.

"Does this really need to take all day?" Mai said. "Honestly, Jun—"

But her words were cut off abruptly. Scout felt a rush of wind stirring her hair, and the moment she turned to look towards Mai, Jun was already there, her hand closing around her sister's throat.

She waited until her sister's face went from red to purple before throwing her to the ground.

Then she turned to face Shi Jian.

26

JUN'S FACE was as inscrutable as always. But her hands were flexing in and out of fists, and her body language was shouting just one thing: determination.

Shi Jian sighed as she stood up, stepping over Daisy's crumpled form. She flicked the hem of her cloak as if letting it brush over Daisy would sully it.

She raised her right arm in its horrid red sleeve and made a come-at-me gesture.

"Jun," Mai tried to squawk, but what came out of her throat was little more than a whistle of sound, easily ignored.

Jun didn't charge at Shi Jian; she advanced deliberately, one step after another. Scout supposed this was a fighting stance, but to her, it looked like a dance, it was so light and precise. When Jun was just over an arm's length away, she started circling Shi Jian, hands up but loose, not in fists.

Scout had always thought passionate rage was Jun's defining feature, but there was none of that in her now. She was a creature of infinite patience, waiting for Shi Jian to make her move.

Shi Jian grinned as if this were all a big game. Then, fast as a snake strike, her right hand fired forward to catch Jun in the chest.

The movement was too fast for Scout's eyes to follow, but Jun didn't seem to have that problem. The next moment both of their bodies were still, Jun had a hold of Shi Jian's wrist, pulling her arm to full extension and using it to control her, to pull her further away from Daisy.

Shi Jian's foot snapped at Jun's kneecap, and Jun let go but resumed circling.

Shi Jian's grin was gone.

Scout led the dogs closer so that she could kneel beside Daisy. Gert huddled close behind her and Shadow was shaking like a leaf, but they shared Scout's concern for Daisy. When they reached her side, Shadow began earnestly licking at her face.

"Are you okay?" Scout asked. Daisy looked up at her with blood-shot eyes. This was more than the eyes of someone who had missed a few nights of sleep; her left eye had what looked like a spidery clot trying to wrap around her iris.

"Help me up," Daisy said. She had to close her eyes to focus her energy on getting the words out.

"I don't think you're ready for that," Scout said.

"Up," Daisy said again, trying to push her own weight up with trembling arms. Scout hooked the leashes around her wrist so she could use both hands to help Daisy sit up and lean against her.

Daisy took a moment to catch her breath, then looked up at Shi Jian and Jun, still circling each other. Shi Jian was being more cautious now.

Suddenly the dogs started barking, and Scout saw that Mai had gotten back on her feet and was waving at her ship.

Then she saw the guards at the base of the ramp trying to get their hostages—her friends—back inside the ship.

"Stop!" Scout shouted and released her dogs. They ran to pull at the pants legs of the guards. Gert tripped hers, sending her down on her butt with a whoosh of chaff from the dry grass. Shadow was too little for that, but he was twice as tenacious. The guard he was attached to was barely able to take a step.

The guard raised his rifle, prepared to strike Shadow with the butt of it, but before Scout could even shout another alarm, Arvid and his squad had boiled up out of the grass. One of them hit the guard in the side of his head with her own rifle. Two more kept the fallen one pinned down on the ground. Arvid and the others stood at the base of the ramp to keep more guards from coming out.

A sudden scream drew Scout's attention back to the fight. Jun was stumbling back, clutching the side of her face as she shrieked.

"What happened?" Scout asked.

"Shi Jian nearly got her," Daisy said.

"Nearly?"

"Jun dodged to avoid being punched, but not enough. Shi Jian's fist brushed her cheek."

"That contact was enough?" Scout said. "She's enhanced, like you."

"Not like me," Daisy said. "She's more advanced than me. But not as much as Shi Jian."

"She can't win this," Scout said. Jun had stopped staggering back and seemed to be having a hard time staying upright. She was clutching her cheek and taking deep breaths, but not even looking up at Shi Jian advancing on her.

"Not alone," Daisy said. "Help me up."

"You can't fight her again!" Scout said. "What if she hits you again?"

"I need to give Jun an opening," Daisy said. Her words were coming more easily now, but she was nowhere near ready for a fight. "Please, Scout. She can't take us."

Scout bit her lip but saw no other choice. She slipped her arms around Daisy's chest and helped her to her feet. Daisy's enhanced body was incredibly heavy, and she didn't seem to be taking any of her own weight. Scout's legs trembled, and there was a moment when she was afraid they would buckle, and she would be crushed under Daisy's collapsing body.

Then another pair of arms wrapped around her, helping her the last bit of the way.

Malcolm.

"You're not going to get a better opening," he said to Daisy.

Daisy nodded. Then she bent forward, focusing all of her energy, and sprinted toward Shi Jian.

Shi Jian had just been reaching out to close her hand over Jun's throat. Jun, still holding her cheek, was just managing to look up at her but still seemed incapable of real movement.

But Shi Jian hesitated, looking back with only the barest turn of her head to see Daisy coming her way. The corner of her mouth curled up as she deemed Daisy no real threat.

But she turned her attention back to Jun just a fraction of a second too late. Jun had her by the wrist again, but this time, instead of pulling Shi Jian's arm straight out, she twisted it around behind Shi Jian's own back. One of Jun's feet swept both of Shi Jian's out from under her, and she fell with a shriek as Jun maintained the hold on her arm.

Daisy helped force Shi Jian to the ground, which seemed convenient for her because the moment they had her down, she rolled away to lie on her back, looking up at the sky.

Jun climbed onto Shi Jian's back, pulling something from her belt with the hand that wasn't pinning her arm. She fired it into the back of Shi Jian's neck. But it wasn't any sort of sedative; it was an energy net that wrapped around Shi Jian's entire body.

Like the cuffs the galactic marshals used, it tightened every time Shi Jian struggled. But she refused to stop struggling.

"Is that going to kill her?" Malcolm asked.

"Probably not," Jun said, putting the tool back in her belt.

"Pity," Malcolm said.

"Jun Tajaki, you are dead to me!" Mai yelled hoarsely. She was standing midway up the ramp of her shuttle, and the ramp was starting to ascend. "You're dead to the whole family!"

"I always was!" Jun shouted back.

Mai reeled as if those words truly hurt her, but then her anger returned. "You just wait until Julius and Augustus hear about this. It doesn't end here!"

Jun just gave her a wave goodbye. Then the ramp was closed, and the shuttle engines started to whine to life.

"That was something," Emilie said as she and the Malini sisters walked over to where Scout was standing with Malcolm and Jun. The dogs followed along behind them, both running to Daisy to sniff and lick at her before flopping down beside her. Daisy raised one weak hand and rested it on Gert's massive head, which was lying on her stomach.

"I'm sorry for what was done to you," Jun said to Malcolm. "My family has been trying to modify my behavior since I was a toddler. I know how it feels to be driven by emotions that aren't even yours. I should have fought harder, sooner. I just… couldn't."

Mai's shuttle lifted off of the grass and shot up into the sky. As they all watched the last shining pinpoint of light from its fuselage fade into the blue, another pinpoint formed, growing larger until another shuttle settled down just where it had been on the grass.

This shuttle was nowhere near as lovely as the Months'. It looked only a shade newer than the vestige of Amatheon's past that Scout and the rebels had flown in on.

"The governor," Malcolm said, pointing at the seal of office before it disappeared from sight as the ramp lowered.

"I called them," Joelle said, raising her chin as if waiting for her father's temper to flare.

"Good call," he said.

"We needed backup," Joelle said. "I guess he got here a little too late."

"It was still a good call," Malcolm said. "We're past due for a discussion."

"Is there another ship up there?" Scout wondered, staring so hard up into the sky that her vision started to swim. "How did Shi Jian get here? And if she came with others, why aren't they trying to rescue her?"

But no one had an answer.

27

GOVERNOR TONY SMITH stepped out of the shuttle, accompanied by a phalanx of Planet Dweller soldiers and a woman in a rich red dress that Scout recognized at once.

"Rona," Scout said. "I never thought I'd see you here."

"Scout Shannon," Rona said with a smile. "I am Bo Tajaki's envoy to this world. I'll be working with the governor and upper management in orbit to facilitate the changeover."

"So the court case is done?" Emilie asked.

"Indeed. Bo Tajaki is now ward of your world. You will no longer be isolated from the rest of the galaxy," she said.

"And the tensions here?" Geeta asked. "The war?"

"The governor and the upper management in orbit have already declared armistice. We just need to speak to one more person…"

"Me," Malcolm said, stepping forward to extend a hand. "Malcolm Haley. I speak for the rebellion, such as it is."

"Mr. Haley," the governor said, shaking his hand. But the look on his face was grim, guarded. "We have much to discuss."

"He didn't kill your daughter," Scout blurted out, startling them both.

"What?" the governor asked.

"Ruth. I was with her when she died," Scout said. "I didn't tell you before."

"The compound she was in was collapsed with explosives," the governor said. "Everyone inside was buried. The air was gone by the time my crew unearthed it. How did you survive?"

"I was the one who blew it up," Scout said. "When I left, after the coronal ejection storm. Everyone else was dead, and I couldn't dig that many graves, so I buried the whole compound. It felt like the right thing to do at the time. I didn't realize I was burying a lot of evidence and creating confusion. I'm sorry."

"But, how did Ruth die if it wasn't in a cave-in?" he asked.

"Poison," Scout said. "Small doses over long periods of time. You must have seen she was getting ill."

"Yes, but she always just said she felt tired," he said. "But how… Clementine."

"Yes," Scout said. "She wasn't just a street kid that your daughter happened upon. She was sent to infiltrate your family. Although why she killed Ruth and not you, I don't know."

"But she was just a kid, barely even twelve."

"There are more," Scout said. "Planet Dweller and Space Farer kids both. Designed to infiltrate and assassinate because who suspects a kid, right?"

"Can this be true?" the governor said, looking to Malcolm, who just shrugged.

"I'm afraid it is," Rona said. "Mr. Tajaki was told they were going to be employed as spies. When he learned the truth, he canceled the program."

"Far too late," Scout said.

"I can tell you all about it," Daisy said. She tried to sit up, failed, then let Gert help pull her up. "I was trained as well. I escaped, but so far as I know, I was the only one."

"And Bo Tajaki was behind this?" the governor asked, shooting Rona an accusing look.

"No," Rona said, raising her hands in self-defense. Then she pointed to Shi Jian, still struggling against her ever-tightening bonds, although her movements were much smaller now. "It was her."

"This is all very confusing," the governor said.

"We can explain all of it," Scout said. "Or as much as we know." She didn't even want to get into everything they still didn't know about Shi Jian. "For now, you should take her into custody."

"Not down here," Rona advised. "Take her up to the ship in orbit. The facilities there are state-of-the-art."

"Yes, of course," the governor said absently. Then he looked back to Malcolm.

"You didn't kill my daughter," he said.

"No," Malcolm said. "I did rob a lot of your trains."

The governor smirked. "They had my seal on them, but I had little use for most of that. My council members insisted on a level of opulence to state dinners that I found superfluous. I hope you all enjoyed it, anyway."

"My father is going to need a few days before you start talks," Joelle said, standing at her father's elbow.

"What's this?" the governor asked.

"He's been under the influence of strong pharmaceuticals," Joelle said. "The Months used them to control him, or at least to provoke him in directions they found convenient. We're tapering him off. The last effects should be purged in ten days or so. Then you can negotiate with the real Malcolm Haley."

Malcolm blinked and wiped at his eye, grumbling something about the chaff in the air.

"As long as you don't continue plotting for violence, I can give you time," the governor said.

Jun helped the soldiers load the bound Shi Jian onto a floating bed, explaining how to shut down the net when the time came.

"What about her?" the governor asked.

"Yes, what about her?" Malcolm agreed. "She's a puzzle. I'm not sure how complicit she was in everything that happened here. In what was done to me."

"She seems to be an ally now," the governor said.

"Perhaps not to be trusted," Malcolm said.

"She is a member of the Tajaki trade dynasty," Rona said. "She must be treated as such."

"What does that mean?" Scout asked.

Rona stroked her bottom lip as she gave that some thought. "She will be a guest of Mr. Tajaki on the ship in orbit. As he is not currently in residence, she can be given his quarters for her own use."

Jun, having heard her name, had walked over. She gave a little nod, as if she found Rona's suggestion acceptable.

"She'll be confined to those quarters, I trust?" the governor said. "She and her sister did a lot of dangerous, life-threatening meddling here, and I'm not prepared to take just her word that all of that was on her sister."

"Of course not," Rona said. "The head of the dynasty will be informed, and the family will take it from there."

"Confined to quarters," Jun said sadly.

"She also may be under the influence of behavior-changing drugs," Daisy said.

"Our medical staff will look into that matter," Rona promised.

"She needs a dog," Scout said.

"Excuse me?" Rona blinked in surprise.

"A companion. To help in her recovery and to make the confinement tolerable," Scout said.

"My brother has taken in strays from all over the capital," Joelle said. "If you stop there before going up into orbit, she can take her pick."

"Does she even deserve that? It sounds like a gift," the governor said.

"It will help in her recovery," Scout insisted. "She's been through a lot. I think a lifetime's worth. It will help."

"We could use her on our side," Daisy said. "Her sister isn't going to just walk away from all this."

"That's likely true," Rona said.

"Very well," the governor said. "But she'll be under guard every moment she's on the ground. I don't want someone like her running loose over my planet."

Rona signaled for two of the soldiers to bring Jun on board the ship. Jun didn't say a word, but the look of fond gratitude she gave Scout was more than enough.

"Now, what about you two?" the governor asked, and Scout realized he was talking to her and Daisy.

"What about us?" Scout asked, afraid that he was going to start blaming them for Clementine.

"You two have been tangled up in a lot of things that need to be untangled as we move forward, a united Amatheon surface and space. We could use you in the capital."

"As in… you mean a job?" Scout asked.

"In the capital," Daisy repeated almost wonderingly.

"Yes," the governor said. "I have plenty of space in the governor's palace, but if you'd be more comfortable with a place of your own, that can be provided as well."

"As you well know, Mr. Tajaki will always supply you with anything you require," Rona added.

Scout didn't know what to say. She had never given a moment's thought to what would happen next.

She realized with a start that she had never expected to make it to the other side of all this.

"I think I need some time," she found herself saying.

"Of course," the governor said. "Take all the time you need. I'll be in touch."

"Here," Rona said, handing Scout a wrist communicator. "In case you need to get in touch with me, or the governor, or Mr. Tajaki. Or anyone else, for that matter."

"Thanks," Scout said, strapping it to her wrist. It was nice to have stuff again. Besides her hat.

"And you?" the governor asked Daisy.

Daisy was looking down at the grass between the feet she had crossed in front of her. She was leaning heavily on Gert, but the sturdy dog didn't seem to mind or even really notice. Shadow was lying beside her, his nose on the bottom of her foot.

"I need time as well," Daisy said at last, looking up at everyone standing around her. "But I would like a ride to the capital."

"Certainly," the governor said. "Shall we?"

"I just need a moment," Daisy said. Malcolm extended his hands to help her to her feet, then to limp over to Scout.

"Are you sure you're going to be all right?" Scout asked.

"Yeah," Daisy said. "I need nutritive fluid, but Rona can get me some of that, I'm sure."

"You're going to the capital?"

"Yes," Daisy said. "I want to see some places. The marketplace. The orphanage. My old home."

"I understand," Scout said.

"I'll keep digging into Shi Jian's background," Emilie said. "Get Rona to give you a wrist communicator, too. We should all stay in touch."

"I will," Daisy promised. Then she turned to Scout. "We should meet again, face to face, before either of us gives Mr. Smith our decision."

"I agree," Scout said with relief. "Talk in a few days?"

"Yes. Take care of yourself," Daisy said, giving Scout a weak hug.

"Get well," Scout said. "Don't push things."

"Who, me?" Daisy said, then stepped away to follow Rona up the ramp.

Scout stood with Emilie, the Malini sisters, and Joelle as they watched the shuttle disappear up into the sky.

"Do you think he's serious?" Scout asked the others, her eyes still on the pinpoint of light in the sky.

"About what?" Emilie asked.

"A job? In the capital?"

"Could be exciting," Geeta said. "If you wanted to stay here, that is. Do you?"

"I don't know," Scout admitted, looking down at her dogs, who were once more snuffling through the grass in search of smaller forms of life. "What about you?"

"I don't know either," Geeta said, looking to her sister. "I think perhaps we'll go back to *Amatheon Orbiter 1* first and see where we stand there. If we still have jobs or are even welcome."

"Of course you'll be welcome," Scout said. "If they don't know yet what you've done for all of them, they will soon. Daisy and I will be sure of it."

"I hope so," Geeta said. "I liked my job."

"Me too," Seeta said. "I don't know how you can stand all this... nature."

"Really?" Scout said, enjoying the prickling warmth of the sun on her arms, the oven-hot breezes that ruffled her sweat-dampened hair. "What about Galactic Central?"

"Very good for nature simulation," Seeta said with a smile.

"I'm heading back there," Emilie announced. "Next ship back, I'm on it."

"The data hub of the galaxy," Scout guessed.

"And I barely got to see it," Emilie said. "Barely even scratched the surface of the material the Months would let me have access to. How much more is out there... it boggles."

"Bo Tajaki would be glad to have you," Scout said. "I bet researching Shi Jian would even be a paid position in his household. She duped him, longer and harder than she duped anyone else."

"That she did," Emilie said. "But no more."

"We can take you back to the compound with us," Malcolm said to the three Space Farers. "Tom Tom can take you back up into space."

"Appreciate it," Emilie said.

"And what about you?" he asked Scout.

She looked out over the prairie, then at her dogs chasing first some little animal and then each other around and around the flattened circle of grass.

She could just start walking. Pick a point on the horizon and head towards it. Call for a pickup with her wrist communicator whenever she liked.

Or...

"My rover," she said to Arvid. "Is it still at your compound?"

Arvid nodded. "My niece Bente repaired the damage, made some small modifications. It runs better than ever."

And, Scout was sure, her bike was still stowed in the luggage compartment.

"Take me to it," Scout said, then whistled for her dogs to join her.

								28

UNLIKE DAISY, there was nothing in particular that Scout wanted to
see. She knew people who would be happy to see her, but no one she
was as close to as she was to Daisy, Emilie, and the Malini sisters.

She wanted to think about the choice she was about to make, but
she didn't want to ask anyone's advice about it. She just wanted to be
alone, with her dogs, to think.

The first day she just kept the rover rolling over the prairie,
bypassing all the towns.

When the sun started to set, she parked and let the dogs run and
explore.

All day she had kept a nervous eye on the coronal mass ejection
indicator, but it had never twitched. As she ate her dinner that night,
she traded messages with her friends in space. They were busy,
working with Rona and the governor and their own upper management to iron out the details, but they were certain the danger was past.
Not only would the shield stay around the planet, they had orders
from Bo Tajaki to improve it.

"The color of the sky is going to change slightly," Emilie said to her.
"But when we're done with the improvements, the entire surface will
be safe at all times. The domes can even come off the cities."

Scout didn't know how to respond to that. It seemed like something out of a dream.

But beyond anything she had ever dreamt of. The entire surface, safe. That was really going to change life in the villages and cities both.

She slept in the rover bunk, the dogs curled up close to her. Shadow preferred to be in her arms with his head on her biceps and his back to her belly. Gert, by default, curled up behind Scout's legs.

Scout woke to the familiar feeling of Gert's heavy head on her hip, those brown eyes waiting patiently for her to wake and let the dogs outside.

Scout complied. She ate a protein bar for breakfast, then filled a bottle of water from the sink in the kitchenette. She put on a sun-protective shirt over the rest of her clothes and carefully applied sunscreen to every exposed centimeter of her skin.

Was that, too, going to change? She would have to ask Emilie.

Scout hopped out of the rover and shut the door, but she didn't bother locking it so far from civilization. Then she went around back and pulled her bike out of the storage space.

She gave the bike a thorough check, but everything was in good working order. Even the tires were properly inflated. She swung a leg over, put her feet on the pedals, and started rolling down the gentle slope, the rising sun warm on her back.

She whistled, and the dogs burst out of the grass to fall into step beside her. Shadow looked up at her, ears high and tongue lolling. He would have been grinning if he had been human.

Scout kept an easy pace and stopped in the shadow of a large boulder to wait out the hottest part of the day. The dogs drank down the water she poured into a bowl for them and then flopped down to nap.

If only she had somewhere she was supposed to be, some package or message with her that was her responsibility to deliver, then every-thing would feel just right. Like being home.

But it didn't feel just right, and Scout wasn't sure why. It was more than just the lack of a job; she had spent days wandering around between jobs before. Something else felt... well, not so much wrong as out of alignment somehow.

The heat lulled her into her own doze, and she woke a few hours later to the sound of the dogs trying to corner some small animal in its den under the boulder. Scout had them drink a little more water, had some herself, then went to pick up her bike.

She looked to the west. There was always more west. The north had its mountains, and the south had a river she had never dared cross. The east ended with the major cities along the coast of the ocean, but there was nothing but endless prairie to the west.

It was tempting, to keep pedaling away from everything. But she was never going to find anything out there. The answer she was looking for certainly wasn't out there.

Scout whistled, and the dogs ran to catch up as she pedaled back to the rover.

She reached it just as the last sliver of the sun was sinking below the horizon. The dogs were wiped out, having grown used to spending most of their time lying about.

Whatever Scout decided, the dogs would have to be a consideration. They needed space to run and critters to chase.

But their needs were easy to meet. What did Scout need?

Scout put the bike away, then climbed into the rover. She took one MRE from the stack in a crate near the kitchenette and pulled the string to start the heating element, then filled a tall glass with more water.

She filled the dogs' bowl with kibble, and they ate companionably side by side, devouring every last bit before Scout's food was even warm. Gert flopped down at Scout's feet and immediately went to sleep. Shadow licked at the edges of the bowl until absolutely every crumb was consumed before hopping up onto the bench next to Scout and curling up with his head on her thigh.

Scout spooned food into her mouth. She hadn't glanced at the label, but it was some sort of beef in a tomato sauce–type thing that wasn't bad.

She sent Emilie a message asking about the future need for sunscreen.

Emilie didn't answer straightaway. Probably in another of their endless series of meetings.

She thought about messaging Daisy, but she couldn't think of what to say. She didn't want to intrude on what was clearly a personal time for Daisy. Scout didn't think she had ever properly mourned the loss of her sister.

In the end, she just sent a short note: "I hope all is good with you."

Then she went to bed.

She woke when the sky was just barely hinting at something about to change in the east. Something was beeping at her.

Scout sat up, ignoring the dogs' protests. It was her communicator. Rather than sending a message, someone was trying to call her directly.

At this hour? It could only be bad news.

Scout pushed the hair out of her eyes and answered the call.

"Yes?" she asked anxiously.

"Hey, Scout," Tucker said. She could see part of his face on her wrist screen: eyes but not eyebrows, mouth moving in and out of frame as he talked. "I have some news for you."

"Oh no," Scout said.

"Oh, it's not bad," he said.

"At this hour?" Scout asked.

"Oh, sorry," he said. "Wasn't paying attention."

Scout sighed. "What's the news?" she asked.

"Your galactic marshal friend, Liam McGillicuddy, was released from tribunal custody. Some sort of deal was worked out with the Tajaki trade dynasty."

"That is good news," Scout said, perking up.

"He's on his way here now," Tucker said. "He left even before we knew he was free, so he's nearly here already."

"Where's he heading?" Scout asked.

"The same place you met him before. The coordinates are still in the rover's nav system," Tucker said. "He'll be there by tomorrow morning. I hope you're close enough to reach it in time."

"Yes, plenty of time," Scout said.

"Oh, good. Because otherwise, I could send him to your current location…"

"Thanks for the offer, but I'll be there before he will, for sure," Scout said.

Tucker said nothing. It was hard to tell from the fraction of his expression she could actually see, but he seemed very eager to please.

"Have you heard from Daisy?" Scout asked.

"She's been staying with Reggie in the capital," Tucker said. "But I haven't talked to her."

"Has Joelle?" Scout asked. "I'm just curious how she's doing."

"I don't know. Do you want me to ask?"

"No, it's nothing," Scout said. "Does she know about Liam?"

"I don't think so. You want me to tell her?" Tucker asked.

Scout bit her lip. The last time Liam had come, it had meant he was going to take her away. And he had. But is that what he was coming for this time?

Were her options now staying out in the prairies of Amatheon as a messenger, staying in the capital, working for the governor, or going back into space with Liam?

She didn't know for sure what Liam was going to offer her.

But she did know that whatever it was, she wanted Daisy to have all the same options before her before she decided.

"Yes," Scout said at last. "Please tell Daisy. I'd appreciate that. Thank you, Tucker."

"Yeah, of course," Tucker said, ducking his eyes out of frame, so she just had a view of his forehead and floppy hair.

She would never trust him again, not completely. They could never be friends. But she realized that the last of her anger had finally left her. She was okay, her dogs were okay. She could let Tucker walk his own path and she would walk hers. She didn't think they'd ever cross again, but she no longer actively wished him ill.

That was something.

Scout terminated the call, but there was no way she'd ever get back to sleep. Once the dogs had run off some steam, she started up the rover and headed for the rendezvous point.

She didn't reach it until late afternoon. The grass was still flattened from Arvid and his crew, and there were deep indents from where the heavy craft had stood parked around the perimeter.

Scout braked the rover and killed the engine. Then she climbed back down to the back to open the door and let the dogs out for another run.

They leaped eagerly out of the doorway, quickly disappearing into the tall grass.

But they weren't the only ones causing the stalks to sway. Scout stepped back into a defensive posture, hand reaching for a slingshot that was no longer there.

But the grass parted, and Scout saw it was Daisy walking towards her. She wore no hat over her closely cut hair, and her long arms were bare, but her nanites were up to the task of fighting sun damage. She had darkened a bit, her usually Spacer-pale skin now a warm honey color. It made her hair look even more golden, her eyes more brilliantly blue.

"You got Tucker's message," Scout said, jumping down from the rover.

"I did indeed," Daisy said. "There's something for you just over here."

"There's what?" Scout asked.

"Just come and see," Daisy said, waving for Scout to follow her through the tall grass.

They didn't have far to go. A puffy package was lying against a rock, a long parachute trailing behind it. Without the rock, the package might have bounced away in the stiff breeze.

"How do you know it's for me?" Scout asked, wadding up the parachute and shoving it underneath another rock.

"Just here," Daisy said, pointing to the side of the package. "'For Scout Shannon, from a friend who dwells above,'" she read.

"Caleb," Scout said. "He's the Months' majordomo."

"The Months," Daisy said with a frown. "Let me look it over more carefully before you touch it."

"Caleb wouldn't send me anything that would hurt me," Scout said, but she let Daisy examine it, anyway. Better safe than sorry.

When at last Daisy gave the nod, Scout tore open the puffy protective packaging.

Inside was her belt, her boots and pants, and a clear plastic pouch filled with all the things from her pockets.

And resting on top of all of it were her glasses.

Scout gave Daisy a deliriously happy look, then clutched it all to her chest tightly and ran back to the rover to get changed.

"I've felt so naked without this," Scout said as she finally buckled the belt back around her hips.

"You do seem to be missing something without it," Daisy agreed. She was feeling a teapot with steaming water, having already found Ottilie's stash of tea in the highest cupboard.

"I've been feeling out of sorts since we got back here," Scout said. "Not myself. Maybe it's the belt."

"Maybe," Daisy said. "Would you like some tea?"

Scout was about to give a tepid affirmative when Daisy turned to set something on the dining table in front of Scout. "Or would you rather have a jolo?"

"Jolo!" Scout said, wrapping her hands around the bottle. It was so icy cold it made her fingers ache, and condensation was already dripping in great fat drops down the sides. Daisy smiled, setting her teapot and cup on the table and sliding in across from Scout.

Scout took a long swallow of jolo, closing her eyes as the rush of sugar and caffeine coursed through her blood.

"Maybe this is what was missing," Scout said.

"Maybe," Daisy said, as evasively as before.

"How was your time in the capital?" Scout asked.

A twinge of sadness crossed over Daisy's face, but she blinked it away before pouring out her tea.

"It was necessary," Daisy said. "I had to close a chapter before I could open a new one."

"Yeah," Scout said, looking at the bottle of jolo in her hands. Did she have chapters that needed closing?

"That belt is more than a belt," Daisy said, the random comment catching Scout off guard. "It's a badge of office."

"I suppose I shouldn't be wearing it," Scout agreed.

"Well," Daisy said. "I do think it suits you. The belt and the badge and the office, all of it. Have you thought about it?"

"Thought about what?"

"Being a galactic marshal?" Daisy asked, sipping at her tea.

"I hadn't thought beyond maybe going to school," Scout said, "and even that feels impossible."

"It isn't," Daisy said. "Not for you. You're far cleverer than you give yourself credit for, and you have so many people to support and help you."

"The second part is definitely true," Scout said. "Hey, do you think that's what Liam is flying out here to do? To ask me to become a marshal?"

"Probably not that directly," Daisy said. "Like you were sort of saying, it takes a lot of schooling. But what do you think about it? Doesn't it seem like what you've been taking steps toward since the moment you met Gertrude Bauer?"

"It kind of does," Scout said wonderingly. "I wanted to follow her everywhere, all over the galaxy. But she died. Then I wanted to finish her last job. Not technically a marshal job, but still."

"And you named your AI teacher after her. Your mentor," Daisy added.

"I did," Scout said. "Maybe that is what I wanted. I was just too afraid of wanting it and not getting it to actually even think it out loud in my head."

"It's a long path," Daisy said. "There will be lots of points along the way where you could change your mind, follow a different path. But it seems like the logical place to start."

"It does," Scout agreed. She drank the last of her jolo. She could hear the dogs erupt into another sudden chase and knew that they were near, they were safe, they were happy.

"What about you?" Scout asked. "What do you want to do next?"

"I thought that was obvious," Daisy said, fidgeting with the delicate handle of the teacup. "I want to go with you."

"To be a marshal?" Scout asked.

"Or whatever," Daisy said. "Lots of paths, right?"

"That's why you were trying to convince me? But you don't need me. You're smarter than I am and stronger. You'd be so far advanced from me on that path."

"I suppose. But I've been alone all my life, or nearly so. I don't want to be alone anymore. So I've already decided: If you want to work for the governor, I'll do that too. If you want to work in orbit, I can find a place there. Even if you want to stay here and carry on as a bike messenger, I can get a bike of my own. It can't take too long to learn how to do it, right?"

"Well…" Scout said.

"I just know that if I choose anything apart from you and your dogs, I'll be alone. And I think the loneliness might really kill me this time. So I'd like to stay with you. If that's all right. I don't want to impose—"

"Like you could even impose," Scout said, reaching across the table to grasp Daisy's hand. "I don't know if I'll stay the entire path to being a marshal, but I'd like for us to start down it together."

Daisy smiled at her.

"But Daisy, I'm going to make sure that the network of help and support you said I have, that you get one too. You're not going to be alone again, even if we're apart."

"I hope so," Daisy said.

"Now," Scout said, getting up from the table. "Let's go outside. I can spread a blanket on the ground, and we can watch the sunset one last time on our home world."

"And in the morning, we can watch it rise one last time," Daisy added.

"And then Liam will be here," Scout said. "And then everything really begins."

They spread out the blanket and sat down, leaning back on their hands to gaze up at the sky. Shadow and Gert eventually drifted over, Shadow curling up against Scout's side and Gert laying her head on Daisy's thigh.

Scout knew now what had felt out of place before. It was her. She was from Amatheon, but she no longer felt *of* it. There was another place that called to her now.

And that place was the entire galaxy.

NEW SERIES: THE FORGOTTEN PLANET

Coming soon from Ratatoskr Press Books, the new YA sci-fi series THE FORGOTTEN PLANET starts with book 1: Raiding the Forgotten Derelict.

History sleeps beneath them all, but only she sees it.

Lafayette Eloi always knew her parents thought differently from others. They kept their books buried beneath her mother's house. They spoke an old language in the dead of night, whispering behind closed doors and bolted shutters. She grew up in a village where no one was related to her, and she never knew why.

Then, after her mother died, her father came to fetch her. Now she and her mother's dog assist her father in his work. The work discussed in whispers in the dark. The work that had cost Lafayette so much all her young life.

But now she learns just how much her father's work means to their entire world. Only no one knows anything about it. Only her father. And only Lafayette.

Because the work that consumed her father's entire life and her mother's too now nibbles at the fringe's of Lafayette's own life. And she cannot refuse its call.

Raiding the Forgotten Derelict, first book in the new YA sci-fu series THE FORGOTTEN PLANET, available in September 2024 from Ratatoskr Press Books.

COMPLETE SERIES: THE RITCHIE AND FITZ SCI-FI MURDER MYSTERIES

The Ritchie and Fitz Sci-Fi Murder Mysteries starts with Murder on the Intergalactic Railway.

For Murdina Ritchie, acceptance at the Oymyakon Foreign Service Academy means one last chance at her dream of becoming a diplomat for the Union of Free Worlds. For Shackleton Fitz IV, it represents his last chance not to fail out of military service entirely.

Strange that fate should throw them together now, among the last group of students admitted after the start of the semester. They had once shared the strongest of friendships. But that all ended a long time ago.

But when an insufferable but politically important woman turns up murdered, the two agree to put their differences aside and work together to solve the case.

Because the murderer might strike again. But more importantly, solving a murder would just have to impress the dour colonel who clearly thinks neither of them belong at his academy.

Murder on the Intergalactic Railway, the first book in the Ritchie and Fitz Sci-Fi Murder Mysteries.

COMPLETE SERIES: THE TRAVELS OF SCOUT SHANNON

The complete six-book series THE TRAVELS OF SCOUT SHANNON begin with book one, Under Falling Skies.

Scout Shannon's whole family died the day the Space Farers dropped an asteroid on their domed city. Now she lives alone, out in the wild with only her dogs for company. She prefers it that way.

But Scout finds herself at a crossroads. One road leads back to a quiet life snug under the protective dome of a city. The other road leads to a life in the rebellion, a life of adventure and excitement but also danger. Dare she try to find the rebels hiding in the hills?

Then a chance encounter with a stranger from the other side of the galaxy threatens to derail what remains of Scout's life. The entire galaxy awaits her, if she survives the next four days.

"Under Falling Skies", a young adult science fiction novel, set on a remote planet with a distinctly Old West feel. For fans of gunslinging women and young girl assassins. And dogs.

Under Falling Skies, the first book in THE TRAVELS OF SCOUT SHANNON, available everywhere now.

SCI-FI SERIAL PODCAST!

Check out my new monthly podcast of serialized science fiction: THE TALES OF THE CHAI MAKHANI TRIO!

Elyot loathes the massive Commonwealth ships that hover menacingly over his home world of Adghal. He hates the Commonwealth enforcers who harass the populace even more. But with his mother missing and presumed dead, Elyot keeps his head down and strives to avoid notice. And he succeeds until the day two strangers enter his life...

New episodes of this sci-fi serial drop every 1st of the month.

Now streaming on Apple Podcasts, Google Podcasts, Spotify, Stitcher and more. Also available in eBook and print everywhere books or sold. For a complete episode listing, check out the page on my website.

ALSO FROM KATE MACLEOD

Love heists and capers? Then check out my new series, THE VIC HARPER CAPERS. The action starts with the novella THE THIRD POLE JOB.

Vic Harper and her gang retired wealthy from their life of thievery and heists. Whether in a luxury condo overlooking the river in Minneapolis or in a modernist mansion built into the side of a mountain in Colorado, life comes easy now.

Perhaps too easy.

When an old friend asks for a favor his niece, Vic and her mentor Chase Woodward leap at the chance to relieve a little of the boredom. But a quick bit of B&E in a wealthy suburb of Chicago leads to an even greater challenge.

The prize? Nothing much. Just the opportunity to level a playing field for their friend's niece.

But the heist? May prove to be their toughest ever. Because to get to the prize, they'll have to climb a mountain.

And not just any mountain. Their prize waits on the summit of Mount Everest.

THE THIRD POLE JOB, the first novella in the Vic Harper Caper series. For those who love capers, heists and other impossible missions.

Also from Ratatoskr Press, The Witches Three Cozy Mystery Series by Cate Martin, a mix of mystery and magic that begins with Book 1: Charm School.

Amanda Clarke thinks of herself as perfectly ordinary in every way. Just a small-town girl who serves breakfast all day in a little diner nestled next to the highway, nothing but dairy farms for miles around. She fits in there.

But then an old woman she never met dies, and Amanda was named in her will. Now Amanda packs a bag and heads to the big city, to Miss Zenobia Weekes' Charm School for Exceptional Young Ladies. And it's not in just any neighborhood. No, she finds herself on Summit Avenue in St. Paul, a street lined with gorgeous old houses, the former homes of lumber barons, railroad millionaires, even the writer F. Scott Fitzgerald. Why, Amanda can practically hear the jazz music still playing across the decades.

Scratch that. The music really, literally, still plays in the backyard of the charm school. Because the house stretches across time itself. Without a witch to protect this tear in the fabric of the world, anything can spill over. Like music.

Or like murder.

The complete series is out now, and it all starts with Charm School.

FREE EBOOK!

Like exclusive, free content?

To get two prequel short stories to THE RITCHIE AND FITZ SCI-FI MURDER MYSTERIES as well as a bonus prequel novelette to the completed six-book series THE TRAVELS OF SCOUT SHANNON, signup for my monthly newsletter at KateMacLeodWrites.com.

Thank you!

ABOUT THE AUTHOR

Photograph © 2016 Jonathan Conklin

Kate MacLeod has written stories which have appeared in Analog, Strange Horizons and Mythic Delirium, among other places. She is also the author of two young adult science fictions series: The Travels of Scout Shannon, and The Ritchie and Fitz Sci-Fi Murder Mysteries. She also contributes to a serialized science fiction podcast called The Tales of the Chai Makhani Trio. She currently lives in Minneapolis, Minnesota.

Find out more about the author and sign up for her newsletter at KateMacLeodWrites.com.

ALSO BY KATE MACLEOD

Novels

The Slums of the Solar System:

Mitwa

The Mars of Malcontents

The Whole World for Each

Books 1-3 Box Set

The Travels of Scout Shannon:

Under Falling Skies

In Quaking Hills

Among Treacherous Stars

Against Impassable Barriers

Over Freezing Altitudes

At Galactic Central

The Travels of Scout Shannon Books 1-3

The Travels of Scout Shannon Books 4-6

The Travels of Scout Shannon Books 1-6

The Ritchie and Fitz Sci-Fi Murder Mysteries:

Murder on the Intergalactic Railway

Murder in the Skies

Body in the Catacombs

Death on the Summit

An Undiplomatic Murder

A Lethal Betrayal

The Forgotten Planet

Raiding the Forgotten Derelict (Forthcoming September 2024)

Sci-Fi Novellas

The Intergenerational Tree

I Rise into a Daybreak

Caper Novellas

The Third Pole Job

The Twelve Days of Christmas Job

10-Story Collections

Tales of Blood and Ink

Tales of Old Gods and New

5-Story Collections

Tales from Heian-Kyo and Others

Tales from the Edges and Ends

Tales from Forgotten Days

Tales from Ancient and Future Times

<u>Tales from Across Space</u>